A Clue?

I yanked out the third drawer down, and got a squeamish feeling, seeing things Diane had worn next to her body. I scooped them up and shoved them into the garbage bag.

What about the bottom drawer? I knelt on the floor and tugged at the handles. As I thought, it held nothing but junk. I threw out an old swimsuit, a pair of jeans that had white paint splotches, and a once-white tennis cap.

The last thing was an old flannel shirt, also paint-splotched. I picked it up. There was something beneath it. A crazy instinct told me to leave it alone, not to look under that shirt. But I did. And I saw what the shirt had concealed . . . some sheets of paper towel, splotched with brown.

Brown . . . but somehow, shuddering, I knew. This had once been bright red blood! When I moved the towels, gingerly, I saw what they had concealed, and I didn't understand it at all. There was Steve's photo, the eight by ten he'd given Diane some time ago. The glass was smashed.

HOW COULD YOU DO IT, DIANE?

Stella Pevsner

AN ARCHWAY PAPERBACK
Published by POCKET BOOKS
New York   London   Toronto   Sydney   Tokyo   Singapore

An Archway Paperback published by
POCKET BOOKS, a division of Simon & Schuster Inc.
1230 Avenue of the Americas, New York, NY 10020

Copyright © 1989 by Stella Pevsner

Published by arrangement with Clarion Books,
a division of Houghton Mifflin Company

ISBN: 0-671-70897-X

First Archway Paperback printing January 1992

10 9 8 7 6 5 4 3 2

AN ARCHWAY PAPERBACK and colophon are registered trademarks of Simon & Schuster Inc.

Cover art by Kim Milnazik

Printed in the U.S.A.

IL 7+

*With love, for the kids
who choose to live*

How could you do it, Diane?

My sister Diane died five days ago. I still can't believe it. I can't believe she did it.

I ask myself *why*. Why would a fifteen-year-old girl with so much going for her do herself in? Good-looking, smart, popular . . . the things most teens think are important . . . she had all that. Yet she chose to drop out of life. Permanently.

I don't understand it, but then no one does. Mom, Diane's loving stepmother for so many years, is going around dazed and despairing. Dad, Diane's natural father, is beyond heartbroken. I worry about him.

Nell and Ned, the little kids, were whisked away to relatives, so I don't know how much they understand about their half sister's sudden, dramatic death.

It's five days since we found her, two days since her funeral, and it still all seems unreal. There's been so much commotion . . . friends, relatives, classmates, all calling, hanging around. It's like some crazy movie that doesn't know how to end.

Right now I'm in our room . . . mine and Diane's.

Just mine now. I feel wrung out, weary, but I know I won't be able to nap. When I close my eyes I see her again . . . lying there, looking so natural. And then I see her in her coffin, stiff and unfamiliar, and I wish I could wipe that vision from my memory. It wasn't Diane. Not the way she's supposed to be. I want to see her as she was alive, laughing, kidding around.

There's a tap on my door.

I'll pretend I'm asleep so whoever turns the knob and peeks inside will leave me alone. But instead, there's another tap and a soft, "Bethany?" It sounds like it might be Andrea.

It is. We meet at the door and embrace.

"How're you doing?" she asks, pulling away and looking at me.

"I'll make it. I guess."

"It's tough, isn't it." Andrea drops her books on my bed, the closest one, and settles beside them. She's looking very October in her plaid skirt and green sweater.

I sit on the other side of her books. There's a feeling of awkwardness, like not wanting to hang onto the time of the funeral, but not being ready to take up daily life again.

"How's school?" I say.

"Oh." Andrea shrugs. "You know."

"Yeh." There's a pause. I decide I might as well come back to the subject. "Are there any people still downstairs?"

"Several. I didn't recognize them. Your mom said I should just come on up." Andrea scoots around and

2

bends one knee to the side of her. "She looks washed out, the way my mother did. It's really hard, having people around, but then it's bad when they all finally leave, too."

I nod.

"You feel lost and alone. You look forward to sleep, because . . . because he comes back to you in dreams." Andrea's voice is soft, almost as though she's talking to herself. "But then when you wake up, the hurt is even worse because the dream was only a dream, and you know you'll never really see him again in this life."

I give Andrea a swift look as her voice chokes. There are tears in her eyes. Suddenly it becomes real to me, the sudden death of her brother last spring. I hadn't known Andrea then. She and her family moved to our suburb this summer. After we became friends Andrea told me how Joe was killed on his motorcycle. Of course, I felt sorry in a general way, but not until now did I know how shattering a young death in the family can be.

Tears spring to my eyes for Andrea, for me.

"Oh, God," I say. Andrea is crying openly now, and so am I. We reach across the books and hold hands until I get up and bring over the box of Kleenex. We both pull out some tissues. There are just a few left in the box.

Blotting her eyes, Andrea says, "I came over to try to cheer you up, and here I'm just making you feel worse."

"No, you're not. It's good in a way, being around

3

someone who's been through it. People say, 'I know just how you feel' and I want to yell, 'No you don't!' But with you it's different."

Andrea gets up and puts the wadded tissue in the wastebasket. "Are Nell and Ned still at the neighbor's?"

"No, Aunt Pat and Uncle Ned came and got them. They'll bring them back on Saturday."

There's a sound of subdued voices in the hall, and a tentative knock. I go over and fling open the door. Julie and Rebecca are there. They have the watchful look on their faces that I've seen so much lately. A look of *How shall I do this . . . pretend everything's average, make small talk, or go right to the grief?* They will take their cue from me.

"Hi," I say, trying to hit the middle line. "Come on in."

"Hey, Andrea," Julie says. "How did you get here so fast?"

"I skipped last period. It was just study hall."

Rebecca, who has stopped to give me a consoling hug, says, "I wish I could walk out on chemistry. It's awful having it at the end of the day." She goes across to the other bed, sits at the foot of it, and then seems to realize it's Diane's. An expression flits across her face, her body tenses as though she wants to get up again, but she stays. *Does she think it's contagious, suicide?*

There's an awkward pause, then Julie goes over to Diane's desk chair, and I notice for the first time that there's a cherry-colored sweater . . . Diane's . . . flung over the back of it. I have no idea how long it's

4

been there. The sweater twists as Julie sits down and she moves it to the window seat. Her glance lands on some pencil drawings I'd done a couple of weeks ago and left lying there.

"Oh, are these the life sketches we're supposed to do for art?" she asks, picking them up.

"I didn't finish the assignment." How could I?

"This is cute of Nell," Julie says, studying the top sketch. "She's such a doll."

"Let's see . . ." Rebecca goes over. "Oh, darling."

"Too darling, maybe," I say. "Nell's not always all that sweet." I want to snatch away the sketches before . . . but Julie's already gone to the next. Diane. No one says anything.

I remember so clearly the night I did the drawing. Diane was at her desk and I was opposite, sketch pad propped up by books.

"Oh come on, aren't you finished yet?" Diane said after just a few minutes.

"Finished? Give me a break, I've just begun. Hold still, I'm doing your eyes."

The phone rang and Diane leaped up while I squealed a protest. "Why do you have to answer? It may not even be for you."

But of course it was. Diane was a telephone person. Also a loud stereo person, also an earphones-plugged-in-through-the-night person. She talked on and on while I tapped my pencil impatiently. Finally she said, "Tracy, I'll have to call you back, I'm posing for Bethany, some stupid class assignment. No, not in the nude, you pervert. Just the face, my gorgeous face." She laughed at some remark and said, "Oh, shut up."

5

Coming back to the chair, Diane was still smiling. "Tracy said I should pose with a bag over my head. All right, is this the way I was?"

"Tilt your head a little. No, the other way."

I worked as fast as I could, but Diane sighed, drummed her fingers on the desk, moved her shoulders up and down. I got in the basics but the mouth wasn't right. Mostly because it was never in repose.

"Okay, let's stop," I said. "I'll finish it later, since you're so impatient."

"Let's see." Diane reached over, snatched up the sketch, and studied it. "Look what you've done to my nose, you scuzzball!"

"What?"

"This bump."

"It's not a bump. It's just a slight . . ."

"It's a bump. Do I really look that way?" She let the sketch drop to the desk and rushed into the bathroom. I followed and watched while she held up a hand mirror and angled it to pick up her profile in the big mirror. "Oh no! Look at that! It's a bump. It really is!"

"Diane, you're so dim."

"It never used to be that way." She checked her profile from the other side.

"Your face hasn't changed, Diane, and the little teensy rise on your nose means nothing. You're the same raving beauty you've always been, especially the raving part."

She was running her finger down the center of her nose. "Maybe some day I should have it corrected."

"Corrected? You mean plastic surgery?"

"Oh not now or next year," she said, responding to

6

the shock in my voice. "Just some day. When I'm rich and famous and can do anything I want."

I'd never done any more work on the half-finished sketch. I never would, now.

Julie is staring at it, fascinated, as though it has a message from beyond the grave.

There's a rap on the door. It opens immediately. Oh no, Margo. I thought she'd gone.

"Sweetie," she says to me, "could I talk to you a minute?" Her glance takes in the other girls.

"Sure." I get up. "Margo, this is Andrea . . ."

"Oh yes," she says vaguely, "I think we met . . ."

"Right. And Rebecca and Julie." I pause and then explain, "This is Margo . . . Diane's mother."

They murmur hellos, the girls a bit wide-eyed. Margo and I step out into the hall. All she wants is to tell me she's leaving and to say good-bye. We hug, and she says, her voice thickening, "I hope we will always be close, darling. I think of you almost as Diane's real sister." She tightens her hold on me and with a low sob adds, "You're the closest I'll have to my little girl, now."

I pat her shoulder, feeling sorry for Margo, but still hoping this isn't going to turn into another full-blown scene.

It doesn't. She kisses my cheek, says "Promise . . ." and after I murmur I will, she goes down the stairs. I go back into the room.

The girls stare at me, curious, and then look away. Julie hesitantly says, "I guess that was Diane's real mother . . . ?"

"Birth mother."

7

"Oh, right," Rebecca says. "Like, your mother was more of a real mom."

"Margo's very attractive," Julie comments. "In a skinny kind of way. Was she a model or anything when she was young?"

"I don't know. You'll have to ask Di . . ." I stop, shocked. It had slipped out. I forgot for a moment that Diane was dead. "Uh . . . Margo's an interior decorator now, in Chicago."

"You should see her apartment," Andrea says. "All black and peach. It looks like something out of a movie."

Julie's eyes narrow slightly. "How come you saw it?" she asks. Julie is still not ready to accept Andrea as a full member of our group. "Or was it just pictures?"

"I was along one day when Bethany's dad dropped Diane off. Margo wanted us all to hang around, but we couldn't. We were on our way to the Ice Follies."

I get up and close the closet door. It's unsettling to see Diane's things still hanging there. I wonder what we'll do with them.

"I keep forgetting that your father is really just Diane's father, and not yours," Julie says. "You two seem so close. But you said once you can't remember your own dad. It's sad that he died so young." We were silent and then Julie went on. "It still seems strange that Diane came to live with you guys. Usually the mother keeps the kid."

"Oh, get with it," Rebecca says. "Not anymore." She stands up and starts doing waist twists. "Besides, Margo was busy with her career."

We become silent again, watching Rebecca, who has

8

shifted into body stretches. "Why are you doing that?" Julie asks. "Now?"

"The time's always right to keep in shape," Rebecca says, a bit breathlessly. "Seize the moment. You could stand to do some yourself."

Julie makes a face. "Thanks for the hint."

I lean back sideways on my bed. "If I tried to touch my toes I'd collapse. I'm so tired."

"Oh, we ought to leave," Andrea says, looking contrite. "I'll bet you're exhausted. I remember feeling the same way after . . ." Her voice falters and stops.

"No, no, please stay! It's so good to have you guys here instead of . . ." I shrug. "You know."

"I'll bet tons of people have been hanging around," Julie says. "They're so damned nosy when . . . when something like this . . ." She falters. "I mean, any death."

I meet her look. "It's okay to say it, Julie. People want to hear about a suicide." I sit up again. "Why did she do it, how did she do it, where did she do it. . . ."

"Bethany . . ." Andrea looks perturbed.

The other two wait, not willing to ask, but wondering all the same, hoping I'll go on and dish out the real, inside details. The newspaper account had been a simple, standard obituary . . . *beloved daughter of* and so forth. But people talk.

"What are the stories going around?" I ask.

Julie and Rebecca glance at each other. Julie twists her mouth a little and says, "Just that she took an overdose . . . some say pills, some say crack, cocaine, heroin . . ."

"Diane wasn't on any of that stuff!"

9

"I never thought she was," Julie says, "but you know kids, the things they say."

"Adults too, for that matter," Rebecca comments, dropping to the floor and sitting cross-legged.

"So it was just like . . . sleeping pills, tranquilizers?" Julie asks.

"Yeh. We don't know exactly what, or where she got them."

"Well, with your mother being a nurse. . . ."

"She didn't bring stuff like that home!" I say. "She'd never do that, with little kids in the house." But it was the big kid, I thought, not Nell and Ned, who was a danger to herself.

"I heard that Diane didn't leave a note," Rebecca says.

"We never found any."

Everyone's eyes sweep the room, as though a message is sitting somewhere in plain sight, but has gone unnoticed. And I now realize, with a start, that I haven't really *searched*.

"So I guess," Rebecca goes on, "you don't really know why, or anything. Couldn't you just die to find out?" She gulps when she realizes what she's just said. I pretend not to notice.

I'm thinking that somewhere in Diane's desk, tucked into a book or some little container, there could be something she's written. Has anyone looked? I don't think so, except in a general way. I want to start a real search, but not while the girls are here.

I slump again and try to look totally exhausted. They notice and finally leave.

I click the lock behind them. Then I rush over and

open Diane's desk drawer. It's a jumbled mess of Bics and other supplies, old souvenirs from trips and from school events, old letters, old graded papers. There are snapshots, some smeared with ballpoint-pen ink, dating back to when she was a kid, mixed in with more recent ones. There's a cute shot of her and Steve eating watermelon, a couple of her with Steve's Great Dane, one of Nell dressed as a daisy in some kindergarten show, one of me with . . . yuck . . . my freckles in full glory.

I shuffle around and come up with her address book and flip through it. There's nothing here, really, except what you'd expect to find. I shut the drawer.

There are no books on top of her desk. This makes me stop and think. She came home as usual on Friday. She always brought books and homework assignments for the weekend even if she didn't do much studying. But on that Friday she must not have. *She knew she wouldn't need them . . . ever again.*

Oh, Diane.

My throat feels hard.

Diane, you must have planned it. Why? What made you decide to do it? What unhappiness was so intense that this was the only way you thought you could deal with it?

I sit there at her desk feeling desolate.

Oh, Diane, why did you do it?

How could you do it, Diane?

11

Diane and I got along together right from the start. Of course we were just little kids when we met. I was four and Diane was five. My mom and Diane's dad were "going together" . . . I guess that's the way to put it. "Dating" sounds a bit odd for a couple in their thirties, with one a widow (that was Mom, of course) and one divorced.

Years later Mom told me that both she and Bob were concerned about whether Diane and I would like each other, because each of us was an only child, used to the full attention of the one parent. As it turned out, the idea of having a live-in friend who would be like a sister was about the greatest thing each of us could imagine.

From the very beginning we declared ourselves relatives. I can still remember the look of surprise on a shoe salesman's face when we announced we were real sisters. Isn't it strange how your memory tucks away little things? I thought at the time that the salesman was just overwhelmed at how lucky we were to be related, but he probably was thinking how different we looked.

Diane was about my height, though a year older. Her hair was very dark, and so were her eyes, and she was solid-looking. I had curly red hair. Well, I still have it, but now I wear it long instead of in an Orphan Annie style. My eyes are gray-blue, depending on the light, and I was, and still am, on the lightweight side.

After Bob and Mother got married, he officially adopted me. I was thrilled. I couldn't remember my own father and now at last I had a real dad. Also, I felt it made us more a family, sharing as we did the last name of *Kingsley*. Shortly after the wedding we moved to a new, bigger house. And that's another thing that sticks in my memory. Before we actually moved in, the folks took Diane and me to see the house and they couldn't understand why, upstairs, we both started crying. This was after they pointed out Diane's room and then mine.

Diane, still crying, said, "We want the same room."

At first the folks thought we both liked the bigger one, but finally they realized we wanted to *share* a room. In our minds, that was part of the fun of being sisters.

So we . . . Diane and I . . . moved into one front room and Dad and Mom the other. Dad set up his computer in one of the spare rooms and eventually the other was made into a nursery for Ned. Later on, when Nell came along, Dad turned his computer room over to her and moved all his insurance stuff down to the basement. He divided off his work space and no one was supposed to go into it and mess around. There was a sofa and Ping-Pong table in the other part of the basement, near the washer and dryer, but we didn't spend much time down there. Never did we dream that area would be the setting for the worst event in our lives.

Diane and I really did get along. I'm not saying everything was perfect between us, we did have our differences. Like, I hated the way she'd toss apple cores and other half-eaten fruit into the wastebasket and let it all rot. And she'd yell at little irritating habits of mine, like clicking a pen against my teeth when I was doing homework, or looping a rubber band on two fingers and plucking it over and over when I was talking. Whenever I did that, she'd suddenly shut up and stare at me until I said, "What?"

And she'd say, "Do you have to keep doing that?"

"What? Oh. Why does it bother you?"

"It just does. Okay?"

Other stupid little things annoyed us, but what I'm saying is we basically got along well, even though as we got older we became even more different.

Diane turned from a solid little girl into a strong teenager who was great at tennis, good at golf (Dad taught her how to play when she was about ten), a good student, but not Honor Roll. Every year she got better-looking and more popular. Diane liked to have lots of kids around her, and if no one was at the house, she was tied to them by phone.

I became taller, stayed slim, disliked sports, loved ballet and drawing. I was a top student, without any great effort on my part. I mean, I studied and did all the homework and extras, but didn't exactly burn myself out over it. I preferred to be around one friend and didn't particularly like hanging on the phone.

Our folks (we always thought of them as "ours," not her dad and my mother) handed out praise for whatever either of us did well, so there wasn't any pressure laid on us and we weren't rivals.

Now I'm wondering, though. Did grades mean more to Diane than she let on? Did she resent the fact that she had to work hard to do what I seemed to toss off? But even if she did, that wasn't enough to make Diane kill herself. Could it have been because of the breakup with Steve? Or that business with Max? What was it, Diane? Couldn't you at least have given us a reason?

It's Friday again, just a week since Diane did it. The funeral was on Monday, and there were two or three days of people in the house. Then yesterday, Thursday, it dwindled to just our family and a couple of relatives. It was decided that we'd all go back to work or school today.

"Friday is a good day to plunge back into life," Grandma Gwendolyn said. She's Diane's grandmother and is staying on for a couple of days. "Let people say what they have to say and get it over with. Then you'll have the weekend to recover. By Monday, people will not talk so much, because they'll have begun to forget. That's the way people are."

So here I am on Friday morning, looking in the closet, wondering what to wear, seeing Diane's things still hanging on the right side of the closet.

Her shiny tweed jacket. I can picture her wearing it,

sleeves pushed up, shirt collar underneath pulled up the way she always wore it. And I can see her, jacket open, hands thrust in pants pockets, her head tilted back, laughing. Diane laughed a lot. She was a happy girl.

I shake my head to clear away the image.

What shall I wear?

Not a good, special event dress. Not a dress at all, probably. But jeans? No, not jeans. They'd look too *it-doesn't-matter*.

So what shall it be? I shove clothes back and forth, glance at my watch. I'm behind schedule. I grab a pair of pants, slide into them and button on a shirt. Pale pink, not too cheery, not too sad. I knot a natural wheat-tone sweater around my neck. I am clothed to face the world. But my mind trembles.

School was bad, especially when my friends weren't around to run interference.

Kids eyed me from a distance, usually a clutch of them, heads dipped down like hens picking up kernels. Occasionally they'd glance at me, and then there'd be more head dipping.

One or two girls came up and said they were sorry about Diane, and looked as though they expected something more from me than, "Thank you." I walked away.

A solitary kid walking down the hall would eye me until he or she got close, then avoid eye contact and look away. I could almost feel it, though, after we'd passed, the look back at me, as though there was something to be learned from the way I walked.

16

The teachers must have gotten together and decided to say nothing. It helped. In every classroom, after the first few minutes, the tension would ease as the teacher plunged into the subject. By afternoon, I actually forgot myself and raised my hand in history but the teacher called on someone else.

During school my mind was distracted, but the weight of Diane's absence hit me as I was going home. She wouldn't be there. She would never be there again. I wished I could fast-forward my life to months ahead, when surely the pain would have subsided.

Although Mother had gone back to her nursing job at the hospital and Dad to the insurance company, I didn't have to hurry home to be with Nell and Ned because they wouldn't come back until tomorrow. There was no place else I wanted to go, though.

Grandma Gwendolyn seemed glad to see me.

"Hello, darling, come have a cup of tea with me," she said, starting to get up from an armchair in the living room.

"I'll get it," I said, putting down my books. "How are you, Grandmother?" I always called her that, because I'd known her so long and she always treated me the same as Diane.

"Oh . . ." She shrugged. "Making it through the day." There were shadows under her eyes and her face seemed to have wasted a bit.

"Many calls?"

"Not so many as before, praise the Lord."

"They'll taper off," I said as I headed for the kitchen. The teapot was on the kitchen counter, and when it was ready I carried it and the cups and saucers in on a tray, poured the tea, and sat on a chair opposite Grandma.

"I suppose all eyes were upon you today," she said.

"Pretty much so."

"People are curious. When there's a death, there always seems to be the question, "How is she . . . or he . . . or they . . . taking it?" She sighed. "As though it matters."

"Really." I took a sip of tea. It could have been hotter. "I guess it's like when there's an accident and traffic's tied up for miles, from people gawking."

"Yes, the grisly does seem to have an attraction."

"Anything from Aunt Pat? Are Nell and Ned coming home tomorrow for sure?"

"Yes, she called. They'll be here at about ten. And my train leaves at noon, so I'll get to see them."

"Couldn't you take a later train?" I knew they went into the city every couple of hours, and the ride wasn't more than forty-five minutes.

"No, I think it's best if things get back to normal for the little folks' sake. My being here would just prolong the situation." She smiled. "Besides, I have to turn Nell's room back to her."

"You could sleep in my room." *In Diane's bed.*

A little expression flicked over Grandma Gwen's face, but she said normally enough, "Oh no, I think it's best for me to go." Now the pain was in her eyes, as though it had to settle somewhere.

We were silent for a few moments and then she said, with some hesitation, "Bethany, was Diane . . . was Diane an unhappy girl?"

"Unhappy? I wouldn't say so." I stirred my tea. "As

18

we all know, she had her moods. Sulking around, or else getting furious and saying whatever came to her mind. But she got over things faster than the people she yelled at. Like me. Or her friends. Or Dad."

"You don't think there was any special pressure put on her"—she hesitated—"here at home?"

"No, not any more than . . ." I frowned, remembering. "Do you mean that thing about a month ago? When Diane was grounded for the weekend?"

"Margo did mention it to me. That Diane wasn't allowed to come into the city even though Margo had been given some passes for the theater."

"But Diane didn't really care. She made a major scene but she told me later that she was glad she'd got out of going . . . that the play sounded like a big nothing."

"Perhaps she was putting on a brave face."

Diane? I thought. *That wasn't her style.* "I honestly don't think she minded."

"You're probably right. There must have been other things." She smiled bravely. I picked up the dishes and took them to the kitchen.

Other things at home? Was Diane's grandmother trying to lay the blame on my parents? It was unfair! I wanted to say so, but she hadn't actually made any accusations. Not in so many words.

Was it some person's fault, though, I wondered? Did Diane do it because of something said or done? If so, who? And what? The cups shook in their saucers as I set them down. Who was responsible? What was the cause? I knew I would have to try to find out.

3

It's Friday night, and mercifully we're alone. No neighbors, no friends, just Mom and Dad and Grandma Gwendolyn and me. It would be easier if Nell and Ned were here, though. They'd provide some distraction, the way little kids do, so everyone could zero in on them and not have to make adult conversation.

Dinner is difficult. We're still eating leftovers from the things people brought, not because they have any appeal, but no one wants to go to the grocery store. It would seem like such an . . . I don't know . . . an ordinary thing to do, like *hey, it's all over, we're back to regular routine. Don't let me forget the bread and apples.*

The meal finally ends. I insist on doing the cleaning up. I don't mind. I have a special routine for clearing the table, getting rid of the garbage, stacking the dishwasher. It used to drive Diane nuts. She just wanted to shove everything out of sight any old way. She didn't even put Saran Wrap over leftovers in the refrigerator.

I wonder if everything I am going to do from now on will remind me of Diane. I hope not. I mean, I don't want to forget her . . . how could I? But I wish everything didn't make me think of her. It's been so wearing, these days since it happened. I feel dragged out, as though I carry weights on wrists and ankles. Like Diane did sometimes, when working out. There, I'm doing it again.

Instead of fighting it, I let my memory wander back to her and the day it happened. I've already gone over it so many times.

I came home that Friday afternoon a little after three. I took my books upstairs to our room, and saw that Diane wasn't there, which wasn't at all unusual. On days when she doesn't have to check in for baby-sitting Nell and Ned she often has cheerleading or something.

After I'd been in the room a while I decided to take some jeans and tops downstairs to wash them. I remember almost taking Diane's coffee-colored cords, too, that were heaped on the floor, but I was afraid I'd shrink them because they were new and hadn't been washed.

I went down to the first floor and then on to the basement stairs. When I was going down I could tell the overhead light was on, and then I saw that Diane was across the room, lying on the old brown couch. She was lying on her side, eyes closed, and she was sucking her thumb. That was an old childhood habit, something she did only when she was really upset about something.

I remember being surprised that Diane was home

21

this early and wondering why she'd come down here to take a nap. And then thinking that maybe she'd gotten in trouble for cutting class, a thing she did now and then. Or maybe she'd had a fight with someone.

Diane is intense. She makes a big thing of every little argument with any of her friends. *Was intense.* I can't make myself put Diane in the past.

Anyway, when I saw Diane stretched out on the couch downstairs, I was annoyed at her for acting like such a baby, with her thumb in her mouth. I gave her a look, went to the washer, threw in my clothes and the soap, and turned it on to warm wash, cool rinse, as usual.

Then I walked to the stairs, swung around and said, "Diane, you're not asleep, so stop pretending."

I turned back to the stairs but it seemed like a cold hand touched me. Made me turn and look at Diane. Something about the way she was . . .

I took a few hesitant steps toward her, beginning to fear, but still . . . you know. When I got near her I was about to say, "C'mon, Diane . . ." when I saw that her eyes weren't all the way closed. There was a slit of eyeballs showing, and they looked glazed. Her thumb wasn't all the way in her mouth, either. A little thread of spittle had run down her chin.

And suddenly I knew! And that cold hand that had just touched my shoulders before now grabbed hold of me like a giant hook.

Then I wheeled and dashed for the stairs. I stumbled and scraped my shin but I didn't realize it then. And I heard a voice screaming . . . mine . . . and then

I reached the top of the stairs and Mother had just got home, and the kids were there, too.

"Diane!" I screamed. "Diane's . . ."

With a panicked look on her face, Mom brushed past me and clattered down the stairs. By the time I got to the couch she was at Diane's side, shaking her arm, and when she turned to look at me her face was absolutely white.

"Mom . . . no . . ." I said. "No! She's not . . . !"

Mom looked at me, wide-eyed, like an animal in a trap, and then she made an awful deep-throated sound, like a moan, or a howl, and I backed away, staring at Diane. Dead. She was dead.

Suddenly Mom turned and tore to the stairs, pushing Nell and Ned aside. Halfway pulling herself up by the railing, she made the turn into the kitchen. I grabbed the kids by the hands and yanked them along with me. Nell, terrified, started screaming. I guess I was yelling, too.

Mom, practically hyperventilating, crouched over the kitchen counter, punched numbers on the phone, and gasped out to the operator to send the paramedics right away. She hung up and leaned onto the counter, trying to breathe. Then she dialed Dad and didn't say what happened, just told him to come home at once. I guess she mentioned Diane, that something was wrong.

I don't know where Ned was, but by this time Nell was all but hysterical, and I picked her up and tried to shush her. In just a few minutes it seemed, the paramedics pulled up, and I guess Mom went downstairs with them. I know I didn't. They were carrying a lot of equipment, but then one guy came up with the same equipment and took it back to the ambulance.

Loretta Simmons from next door and the Caldwells from across the street saw the paramedics and rushed over to find out what was going on. A police car pulled up and the two officers, seeing us clustered at the top of the stairs, went on down to the basement.

I stood there, feeling numb and yet shaking, holding the whimpering Nell, her wet face against my neck. More neighbors had collected and I could hear the newcomers asking what had happened, and no one really knowing.

Some guy brought Mom back upstairs . . . she looked about to pass out, and then the paramedics came up, carrying Diane on some kind of stretcher. She was all covered up. Dad got there just as they were about to carry her out, and he let out a yell, and Mom and the medics and the police all clustered around him. Dad looked as though someone had taken a punch at him, his eyes were stark and unbelieving.

He made them put down the stretcher so he could see Diane. Nell started screaming and wriggled out of my arms, and rushed over to see, too. I went to get her and saw Diane's face. Her eyes were all the way closed now, and someone had wiped off her chin. She looked . . . what shall I say? Not dead, but not just sleeping, either. Diane's face, even in sleep, was always rosy-flushed, and expressions would flit over her face. Now her face was definitely not rosy and there were no flickering expressions. There never would be again. I couldn't believe this was real.

After they took Diane away—and this made Nell yell even louder: "Where are they taking my sister? I want Diane!"—Dad came into the kitchen, looking like a body without any person in it. His eyes were staring, unfocused. He didn't seem to notice when Loretta took the kids to her house, Nell still screeching and trying to pull away.

"How?" he said, to no one in particular. "Why?"

"Sir," a policeman said to him, "would you sit down for a moment?" He turned to Mom. "And you, too, ma'am." The three of them sat at the kitchen table. I stood behind Mom, my hand gripping the back of her chair.

"I know this is a great shock and a terrible tragedy," the officer said. "I'm sorry I have to do this, I know it's hard for you, but I'll try to be brief." He paused. "Is it all right, do you think you could just answer a few questions?"

Mom gave a little nod. I was glad I couldn't see her face. Dad still looked absolutely stunned.

The officer opened his clipboard. "First, who discovered the . . . Diane?"

I found it hard to speak up. "Me. I did. Only I didn't know . . ."

"How long ago was that?"

"I don't . . . maybe a half hour . . . ten minutes . . . I don't know."

The officer glanced at his watch. "We'll say sometime between four and four thirty. How long before that did you miss her?"

Miss her? What did he mean?

Mom spoke after clearing her throat. "The girls

25

come home at different times. There'd be no reason . . ."

"I see." He scribbled something. "There'll be tests, but we assume she died from an overdose. Do any of you know of any drugs . . . Quaaludes, speed, XTC, crack, in her possession?" He looked at Dad who still seemed to be out of it. Then at Mom, who shook her head, and then at me. His look stayed on my face.

"I've never seen her with anything like that."

"Ever?"

"No."

His steady blue gaze made me think he doubted my word. He looked down to his clipboard, wrote something and said, "We didn't find any container downstairs. Would you mind if Officer Hanks here has a look in her room? Where was it?"

Where *was* her room. Already, Diane was history.

"Right upstairs," Mom said. Her voice sounded hollow. "Bethany can show him the way."

The officer came from the doorway and followed me to our room upstairs. Again, I noticed Diane's cords on the floor. When I'd seen them before, I hadn't known. I picked them up now and put them on the end of her bed, next to an aqua sweater.

"This is Diane's bed," I said. "And there's her desk."

The cop, who seemed young and not too sure of himself, glanced at the bed, then walked to her desk and opened the drawer. Inside it was a mess, as always. After a little bit of moving stuff around, he said, "Nothing in here. By the way, did you happen to find a note?"

"Note?"

He looked at me as though I was really dim. "A suicide note."

"I didn't think . . ." I felt my throat go dry. "When I went downstairs, I had no idea. . . ."

"To the basement? That's right, you were the one who found her." He added in an offhand way, "What made you go down?"

"I went to do some laundry!"

"Oh. And you saw her lying there."

"Yes."

"I see. That your bathroom?" I nodded. "Mind if I have a look?"

I shrugged. As the officer flicked on the light, I sat at the end of Diane's bed and cuddled her sweater against my chest. It gave off a faint scent of Poison, her currently favorite cologne.

"Miss?"

"Yes?" I put down the sweater and went to the bathroom door.

The officer held up a smoke-colored plastic bottle. "Ever seen this before?"

"No. What's in it?"

"Nothing. If it held pills, she swallowed them all." He turned the bottle around. "No label."

I shrank back, as though the bottle still held the power to destroy. "It's just so hard to believe." I felt chilled to the bone. I had trouble breathing.

The cop looked absently around the bathroom and I saw it with his eyes. Facial tissues wadded up on the counter, cotton swabs, tortoise-shell tray holding a bunch of lipsticks, eyeliners, mascara.

27

The cop glanced at the tub, with the shower curtain off to one end, and then he left the room. I glanced at the tub, too, and saw the familiar snakes of dark hair which always drove me wild. "Can't you clean out the damn tub?" I used to yell at Diane. "You're such a slob!"

And she'd say, "What's the difference? Go ahead and shower. It'll all run down the drain."

But it always irritated me just the same. It wouldn't anymore. The next time I showered, those strands of hair would glide away. It would be like erasing the last trace of Diane.

The cop had walked over to the closet now, and was moving clothes around. What gave this stranger the right to handle our things, to nose around? I guess death gave him the right. Diane had lost her right to privacy.

Officer Hanks stooped and looked around on the floor of the closet. "She must have been a dancer," he said, taking in the ballet shoes.

"Those are my things."

"Oh. Sorry." He stood up. "I guess I'd better get this container downstairs." He stopped at the door and turned so abruptly I almost bumped into him.

"By the way, just between us, did your sister ever attempt it before?"

I was taken off-guard but not so much that I fell for his "just between us." Come on, did he think I was that naive? I didn't know what to say, though. Was it illegal to lie about something like this? But how could

28

I tell him? What if Dad found out about that other time?

I shook my head. "Not that I know of."

"Just thought I'd ask," he said. "A lot of times girls don't really mean it, just want to put a scare in the family, a boyfriend, whoever. Then comes the day they do mean it . . . or else they don't get help in time."

I followed him downstairs feeling sick and scared and shattered. Mom half rose and sat me down next to her. Then all eyes were on Officer Hanks as he held up the bottle. "This may be it," he said.

The other cop, still sitting down, took it and looked inside, and sniffed. "Any of you seen this before?" He looked at Dad, who gave a shake of his head that seemed to say, *What does it matter?*

"Ma'am? You didn't happen to bring this home from the hospital?"

"Absolutely not." Mom was looking at Dad, concerned.

"Do you keep any kind of medication around?"

Patiently, Mom said, "Just simple remedies. Nothing unusual. And if anyone has a prescription I keep it locked up, because of the small children."

"Okay. We'll run it through the lab, check it out against what we find in the . . ."

Body. Why didn't he just say it. I couldn't bear to think about what they'd do to Diane . . . when they were checking.

"We'll let you know," the cop said, gathering up his stuff. "It may take a day or two."

29

Mom nodded, got up, and put her hand on Dad's shoulder.

"And folks," Officer Hanks said, pausing at the door, "let me say how sorry I am that this happened. It's just . . . not right for the young to die. It shouldn't be. I'm sorry."

"Thank you," Mom said. She leaned down to Dad, put her face next to his and murmured something. The rest is all a blur, what happened next. I have a memory of people, neighbors, coming inside as soon as the police left, of someone making calls to relatives, and of answering the calls that came one right after another. I remember Hope, Diane's longtime friend, helping with the calls from kids, but most of it's a jumble in my mind.

Then I remember Margo coming in and wailing, "Oh, Bob, our precious baby!" and throwing her arms around Dad. And Grandma Gwen stretched out on Nell's bed, weak and sobbing . . . or was that the next day? I don't know. The talk, the ringing telephone, the human traffic seemed to go on and on.

I'm recalling these things, some very vivid, some a blur, while I finish up in the kitchen, wiping the counter, putting things away, shoving food around in the refrigerator to make room for the still-remaining leftovers.

I start the dishwasher and turn to leave the room, but before I go upstairs there's something I must do. I don't want to, but I know I have to. I must go down into the basement and fish out the clothes I put into

30

the washer one week ago, and which have been lying in it ever since.

I go to the top of the basement stairs, switch on the light, take a step down. Then I turn, switch off the light again, and close the door behind me.

Tomorrow. Tomorrow I'll go down to the washer. I just can't do it tonight.

4

As I make my bed Saturday morning I glance again at Diane's bed and wonder about it. It looks too perfect. Someone must have come in and smoothed the spread, tucked it stiffly in place over the pillow.

I can't remember how it looked that day. Was it a little rumpled? Had Diane lain there first and then gotten up and gone downstairs? It seems important to know this. I want to trace her actions. I want to know what was going through her mind.

No one can help me. Diane was alone in the house. There is no witness.

But why did she go downstairs to die? Could she have done it so we'd find her too late to save her? She'd have known that no one would have gone looking for her right after school, because she often came home late on non-baby-sitting days. It was only by chance that I'd found her so soon. But it wasn't soon enough.

Did she seriously mean to die, though, or just give everyone a scare? Was she hoping to shake up Steve, make him sorry he hadn't taken her back after her breakup with Max? If that was her plan, had she miscalculated the number of pills it would take to put her in a coma, just short of death?

Did she realize what she'd done, down there in the half light of the basement, as the darkness began closing in? Or did she think she was just going to sleep, like a child, with her thumb in her mouth?

I want to go back, to be there, to understand. I want to share my sister's last moments, to let her know there could have been another way. It's no use, though. It's over. Diane's dead and buried.

As I'm standing there, looking at Diane's bed, wondering if it would be worse to keep it and remember, or get rid of it and stare at the vacant space, I hear a car pull up in the driveway. It's the kids coming back.

I've missed the little monsters, but it was good to get them out of the house, away from all the turmoil. It's been really emotional. Along with the crying and wailing there've been a few outbursts between Dad and Margo and her mother. Once, Grandma Gwen told Margo to tone down the hysteria, she wasn't the only one who'd suffered this loss.

It's been exhausting, too, especially for the folks, to have so many relatives and friends and neighbors milling around, talking, talking. And there've been a lot of decisions to make, the kind you never dreamed, a week ago, that you'd have to be making, like funeral arrangements. Burial. Awful things you'd never thought about before.

I hear Nell and Ned come into the house, but

without the usual slamming of doors. A lot of kids can't stand their little brothers and sisters, but to Diane and me, Nell and Ned were welcome additions to the family. They were half brother and half sister to both of us so that made us complete. Sure, there were times when the kids were real pests, when we booted them out of our room, but that was only natural.

I was the one who read to them, played games, helped them with projects like valentines and jack-o'-lanterns. Diane used to give them piggyback rides until they got too big, and then she mostly rough-housed with them. She was the one who showed them how to slide down the banister.

I hear Aunt Pat's voice. I guess I should go down but I don't really want to. Since she's Dad's sister, Pat isn't really related to me, and I'm glad that I don't have to be around her a lot. She's a sports nut and has the complexion to prove it. Her tanned face has the texture of a catcher's mitt.

The kids are coming up the stairs. I wait, door opened.

Ned walks right on past, not giving me so much as a glance. He's carrying a backpack by the straps. I'll go talk to him in a while, when he's a little settled. I wonder what he's thinking, my solemn little brother.

Nell comes along and pauses at my door, wide-eyed, uncertain.

"Hi, Babe." I go forward to meet her, kneel, and pull her close to me. Her body is so small that encircling her, my hands touch my opposite elbows.

I kiss her on the hairline. "How are you?"

"All right."

Nell is small for six, with a heart-shaped face and eyes so blue they look as though an artist created them. Nell, in fact, looks like a Renoir oil of a little girl with blond hair spilling halfway down her back. Sometimes when I see Nell I mentally put her in blue velvet with ruffles down the front, and high-buttoned shoes, instead of the trendy sports stuff she wears, with bright colors and big zippers. Diane was the one who pushed for the *now* look for Nell. She taught Nell current expressions, too, and laughed when she said them in front of her friends.

Nell pulls away from my arms, takes a few tentative steps into my room, and stares at Diane's bed. I wonder how much they've told her. I wonder how much this little kid took in on that fatal Friday afternoon. I wait for her to give me a lead, and am taken aback at what she actually says.

She looks at me with those big blue eyes and says, "When is Diane coming back?"

Oh my God. Doesn't she know about death? Hasn't anyone told her anything? If not, by whose orders? Dad's? Or is Nell just not believing what she was told?

"Nell," I say, "where do you think Diane has gone?"

"She went to heaven."

"Heaven." Well, I think, that's okay. Make pretty images of angels to replace the image of Diane carried out on a stretcher.

Nell goes to Diane's bed, sits on it and bounces a little. "So when is she coming back?"

I wonder if Nell pictures heaven as some sort of super theme park where you have a great time until your tickets run out. "Nell," I say, "Diane's not coming back. She's going to stay there."

With a scowl, Nell announces, "Then I'm going there, too."

My heart thumps, but I manage to say, "Hey, should we go downstairs and see Aunt Pat and tell her good-bye?"

"I already told her. Do you like those dogs?"

I blink at this sudden shift of subject. "Oh, Aunt Pat's bloodhounds. No, I don't."

"They stink," Nell says. "And they lick themselves. Do you want to know where?"

"No. Anyway, you're back home now, and I'm glad." I take Nell's hand and walk her to her room. Then reluctantly I go downstairs. It would be discourteous not to.

I'm in luck. Aunt Pat doesn't stay long. She is on her way to the golf course with the remark, "This good weather isn't going to last forever, so I want to get in a few rounds while I can."

Mom and I glance at each other. I'm thinking, *Too bad she had to miss out on these last few days. So thoughtless of Diane to do it when the weather is so nice.*

I suspect, from her look, that Mom is thinking the same thing. This often happens between us. I don't know why, but it does.

It's Saturday afternoon now, and the house is quiet. Dad had to go to the office to take care of some business that couldn't wait until Monday. Mom and Ned took Grandma Gwen to the train and then they were going to return a coffee maker to Mom's friend, Nancy Schroeder.

"Couldn't she come and pick it up?" I asked Mom.

"She could, but I need to get out more than I need to have company."

I knew what she meant. And I didn't mind staying home with Nell. She looked pale and dragged out and needed a nap. Poor baby, she must have had a hard time, being away so long. A whole week at Aunt Pat's couldn't have been much of a picnic, although there was a teenage sitter they liked, in the evenings.

Nell didn't even make a fuss when the others left and I took her upstairs. I guess she was just happy to be in her own room again.

I lay on the bed beside her and began telling her favorite fairy tale, *Rapunzel*. I hadn't even come to the first *Let down your golden hair* when her lashes gave a final flutter and settled against her cheeks. Her lips quivered then quieted. I leaned over and kissed her, then eased myself off the bed. She didn't stir.

So now I'm in my room and I pick up the envelopes addressed to me, from the batch that came in the morning mail.

I know what most of them will say: Variations of *I'm sorry, I'm thinking of you*. Some people simply signed their names to cards that, to them, said it better than they could. I read each one, from a friend, a teacher, someone who knew Diane in a special way.

I save the one that isn't a card shape until last. It's a regular envelope, with Kevin's return address on it.

Kevin is not my boyfriend. We have never been on what I would call a date. We were in some of the same

37

classes in junior high, but I really didn't get to know him until we both landed on a student citizenship panel. After that we started talking a little, and he confided that he was taking Spanish only because the school had no classes in Latin or German.

I remember being both mystified and impressed. "Why would you want to take such tough languages?" I asked. "Are you going into medicine or something?"

"Only as it relates to chemistry," he said.

"Chemistry? Oh, don't remind me. I just dread the thought of having to take it next year. It's so . . . boring-sounding!"

"Boring? Why would you think that?"

I shrugged. Diane hated it and so did her friends.

"It's fabulous! You should see the experiment I'm doing in my home lab. I'm going to record the steps on a Polaroid as soon as I can afford a camera. I may have to rent one, though."

"We've got a Polaroid you could use. My folks wouldn't care."

He looked at me, amazed. "You'd actually let me borrow your camera?"

"Why not? It just sits on the shelf between birthdays and parties."

"Wow." He slapped his palm against his forehead. "I just can't believe this!"

"Kevin, it's only a camera. Chill out."

From then on, we became now-and-then friends. We didn't hang out together but there was some kind of feeling that linked us. Then this September, the first day of chemistry class, Kevin asked if I wanted to be

38

his lab partner. I said sure, but did he realize what a lost cause I was when it came to science?

"It doesn't matter," he said. "We'll be doing stuff I already know, so I might as well spend time helping you." That's the kind of person he is.

Now I sit here with the envelope from him in my hand. What could he say? Everything possible has already been said. I slit it open and read:

Dear Bethany,
*   I haven't called because I didn't think you needed a lot of talk right now. But I've thought of how you must be, and feel bad for you. I really liked Diane a lot. She was a sweet girl.*

Your friend, Kevin

I read the note again. *She was a sweet girl.*

What a strange way to describe Diane . . . sweet. But then, she had always been nice to Kevin. I guess it was surprising to him, a girl so vivacious and popular, bothering to talk to him the few times he was around our house.

I'd really expected Diane to roll her eyes and make a square-in-the-air sign the first time they met, when Kevin stopped by to pick up the camera.

Steve was there in the family room with Diane, halfway watching a "Fawlty Towers" episode on TV, but restless as usual. The only time Steve wasn't restless was when he was engaged in crunching bones on the wrestling mat. Even now, he was messing around with a basketball, twirling it on a finger.

"Would you just stop that!" Diane yelped as the ball skidded and landed on her chin. "Get that thing out of here!" She threw the ball in back of her, toward the dining room. "You hurt my face."

"Oh, want me to kiss it and make it well?" Steve gripped Diane's chin.

"Cut it out," she said, slapping his hand away.

During all this, I had flopped into a chair and motioned Kevin to do the same.

"So." Steve now took notice of Kevin. "What gives, dude?"

Kevin started describing his chemistry experiment. He was so caught up in his explanation that he didn't seem to realize Steve was taking it all in with a superior little smile.

"That's very interesting," Steve said when Kevin had finished. "Isn't that very interesting, Diane?"

She gave him a dirty look. "It is," she said, sitting forward. And to Kevin, "I never realized that chemistry could . . . like . . . be that interesting."

"Hey, babe," Steve said. "How about the chemistry between us, huh?"

"Oh, you!" She slapped at him again, Steve laughed, she laughed, and I motioned Kevin to leave with me. I couldn't stand to be around Steve and Diane when they acted like stupid jerks.

A little later Kevin went home, and then from the kitchen I heard Steve leave, bouncing the retrieved basketball. Diane came out just as I was putting one of the frozen casseroles Mom had made into the oven.

"I thought you weren't supposed to have Steve in the house when the folks aren't here," I said.

40

"Oh, well. Besides, you had what's-his-name."

"Kevin. He just stopped by to borrow our Polaroid for a day or two."

"Uh huh." Diane picked an orange out of the fruit bowl, tossed it into the air a couple of times, and then started to peel it. "He's kind of cute, in a seminerd way. Your Kevin."

"He's not *my* Kevin. And he's not a nerd. Or a seminerd."

"Actually, I was sort of impressed. The kid is bright."

"Right. Not like that turniphead you go around with."

Diane popped a section of orange into her mouth. "Yeh, Steve is a real zero in the brains department." She started from the room, paused, and said over her shoulder, "But he kisses real good."

I can still hear her laugh.

That was Diane.

It's now the middle of the next week. Diane has been dead for twelve days, two weeks this Friday. I feel like a helpless victim of my own feelings. I don't know when or how they're going to hit me.

For example, only this morning I was in the bathroom getting ready for school when all at once I stopped and stared at Diane's makeup. It's been on the counter all this time, more or less mixed up with mine. But suddenly I got a sick sensation seeing the bright red lipstick she may have smoothed on her mouth the very day she did it.

I reached toward the tube, and gingerly dropped it from my fingertips into the wastebasket. Then I reached for her velvet-black mascara, the blush that was a deeper rose than the one I wore, and dropped them. They made little clicks as they hit each other.

I felt . . . I don't know . . . safer. As though I'd got rid of contaminated objects.

There are times I feel angry, when I want to smash

42

anything connected with Diane. How dare she do this to us!

There are other times when it suddenly hits me . . . *I will never see my sister Diane again!* It's like an icy stab and I crouch in pain, wondering how long it's going to hurt like this.

So many things bring quick tears to my eyes. There are reminders all over the house . . . the sofa pillow she'd cross-stitched for Dad one time at camp, her kindergarten-sized handprint on clay, the top one in a row on a kitchen wall. Photos, of course, a magnet in the shape of a cheerleader on the refrigerator door, her favorite brand of microwave popcorn in the cupboard, her own favorite cereal.

Yesterday morning, in fact, I reached for the kind—corn squares with raisins—I always eat. I saw Diane's sitting there alone on the shelf. Nell and Ned were already spooning up their Wheaties. I hesitated, then took Diane's and dropped it into the garbage. I looked up to see Mom staring at me.

"Why did you do that?" she asked.

"Wh—" I noticed Nell and Ned were also staring, spoons in midair. "Why should we keep it? No one else likes that kind."

Nell waggled her spoon at me. "That was Diane's."

"Look." I felt guilty; why should I feel guilty? "I'll retrieve it." I took the box out of the garbage and slapped it back onto the shelf. "Okay? Everyone satisfied now?" My voice broke. I dashed past Mom who put out a hand, but I shrugged it off.

"Honey . . ."

I grabbed my books and headed for the front door.

43

Again, tears. I angrily brushed them away as I headed down the street.

That's how things are at home. No one is facing things.

A great example was the very first night our family was there alone. We were going to eat in the dining room, as usual. It was Nell's turn to set the table, and she was going around in her dithering way, bringing one plate at a time, singing her song about the bunny in the bonnet. I noticed she'd set six places.

"Nell," I said gently, stooping to her level, "there are just five of us now. You put on too many plates."

She looked puzzled.

"Just Mommy and Daddy and you and Ned and me. Five."

Nell's blue eyes regarded me. "Six," she said.

I took a deep breath. "Don't you understand, babe? Diane is gone. There are just five of us now." How was I supposed to explain it? Why should I have to? Why didn't they . . . the grownups . . . make it clear? It was their duty, not mine.

I stood up and followed Nell to the kitchen. She got six forks out of the drawer. I nudged Mom.

"What?" she asked, when Nell went back to her setting, singing the bunny tune again.

"C'mere." From the doorway, I nodded at the table. "She's setting six places."

Mom went back to the stove to stir some sauce. "Just tell her to set five. Good heavens, Bethany."

"I did tell her. She won't listen. I don't believe that child realizes what's happened, Mother."

"Please." Mom's eyes looked tired. "Leave it alone,

44

will you, Beth? When she's out of the room, just take away a place setting."

"Mom, that's not facing it! It isn't fair!"

"To whom?"

"To them . . . Nell, anyway. I don't know what Ned thinks. No one ever does."

"Why don't you leave the problem of Nell and Ned to your father and me."

"Fine. Fine. If that's the way you want it." I slammed the cutlery drawer shut. "Just don't blame me if they get all screwed up."

Mom kept stirring. Almost to herself she said, "None of the blame is falling on you."

I gave her a startled look and it suddenly dawned on me that some blame might have settled on Mom. Blame from Grandma Gwen? No, probably not, although the poor woman had been beside herself with grief. Margo? If anyone, Margo. The birth mother too busy to raise her own child would be the first to lay a guilt trip on my own poor mother. But Dad wouldn't. . . .

As I was thinking how he'd tell Margo off, he came in the door.

He was trying, really trying to be his usual kidding self with the young ones. He lifted Nell into the air, floated her lightweight body back and forth, and called her his butterfly. Then he set her down, made fists, and putting them on either side of Ned's head, waggled it back and forth. It meant nothing, really, except *Hey, let's lighten up*. Nell was the only one taken in by the charade, though. Ned's smile was forced and his eyes somber.

45

Somehow, Mom managed to remove the sixth place setting before we went in to dinner. Nothing was said, but I sensed Diane's spirit was in the air.

Much later, after the kids were asleep and I'd finished my homework, I wandered downstairs to get an apple and milk. Mom and Dad were in the living room, talking in muted tones.

"What's going on?" I asked.

"Nothing, we were just discussing things," Dad said. "Come sit down for a minute." He patted a space next to him on the chintz sofa. "How are you coming along?"

"Okay, I guess." I lounged beside him. "How are you doing?"

"Oh." Silence. "I'll make it. I guess."

I wished I could be like Diane, who used to ruffle her dad's hair, kid him around. Even if he was annoyed with her she could usually tease him back to a good mood. But I guess Diane wouldn't have tried, in this case. I mean, if I was the one who was dead.

"How's school?"

"Okay."

"That's good."

"Dad . . . have you found out? What Diane took?"

"A barbiturate. Sleeping pills."

"A lot?"

"Enough."

Right. Dumb question. "Do you know where she got them?"

"Do we know, Helen?" Dad asked Mom.

"No, there were none around here. I suppose she got them the way kids get drugs . . . from other kids."

"Should I try to find out?" I asked.

"Save your breath," Dad said. "No one's going to tell you, even if they know."

"I'd like to find out, anyway. Get the damn killer!"

"Beth!" Mom looked startled. "I've never heard you talk that way!"

"Well, no one's ever killed my sister before!" I said, and turned away from Dad, my voice breaking into a sob.

"Honey, honey." He turned me around to his shoulder and put his arms around me. "Feeling that way isn't going to bring Diane back. It doesn't do any good."

"But don't you hate the person who gave her the pills? I do!"

"Bethy, no one forced her. She came home and took those pills and lay down and died. It was what she chose to do."

"Why did she choose to . . . why did she choose to do it?" I was getting his shoulder wet.

"We'll probably never know why. That's another thing she chose to do. She chose not to let us in on the reason."

"Haven't you tried to find out?" I pulled away and wiped my cheeks with my palms. "Haven't you even tried?"

"Hon, you try," Dad said. "I haven't got the heart. I just know I've"—his voice broke and the rest came out muffled—"lost my little girl." He leaned over and put his head in his hands. I knew he was crying.

It broke me up. I mean, Dad . . . !

Mom made a little sign for me to leave, and I looked

back through my tears, from the stairway, to see Mom sitting there beside him, arms around him, face leaning against his shoulder, crooning. Oh God, I felt so sorry for him. And Mom, too. She loved Diane. She really did.

At school, I've tried to avoid going down the corridor past Diane's old locker. The first time I came upon it I could almost see her standing there, surrounded by friends, laughing, flipping back her long dark hair with the hand not holding books. But today I had to face her locker head-on.

A secretary from the principal's office came to my last period study hall and asked to have me excused. She was smiling a little as I joined her, so my first feeling of panic that something else had happened went away.

What she wanted was for me to be there while she cleared out Diane's locker. "I thought you'd be more comfortable if we emptied it while the halls are empty," she said.

"Right." It would be awful, in fact, to have kids staring at us while we did it.

Diane's locker was pretty much of a mess. We put all the books, notebooks, loose papers, blue and white sweater, tennis balls into a box. The empty locker gave me a pang. Another part of Diane gone.

Miss Drake insisted on carrying the box herself out to her car and driving me home. As we drove the few blocks, we filled in time by talking about how warm it still was, though the leaves were turning.

At home, she insisted again that she carry the box,

as though grief had weakened my muscles. When she set it down in our hall I hoped she'd just leave, but before I could say *Thanks,* she said, "Bethany, I haven't had a chance to know you, but I did know your sister fairly well." Her cheeks were slightly pink.

I was tempted to ask if she's the one who passes out demerits and calls home to check out truancy.

"Diane was a girl with a lot of spirit, but she was a doll," Miss Drake said. "A living doll." She realized at once what she'd said and the pink flush in her cheeks became flame-colored.

I pretended not to notice. "Yes, everyone liked Diane," I said. "She had tons of friends."

"Oh, you could tell," the woman said, relieved. "There were so many people at . . . at the . . . wake . . ." She had to say the word. "And it was just, well, heartbreaking . . . such a young girl . . ."

"Yes."

"Uh . . . well, I'll go on back now. Is there anything at all that I can do for you?"

"Thanks, but I can't think of anything."

"All right then. Bye, dear."

"Bye," I said briskly, hoping she'd leave without hugging me. I'm so sick of people I hardly know hugging me. "Thanks a lot."

She went out, but turned. "What about her gym locker?"

"Oh. Maybe you could just get rid of the stuff?"

She looked at me doubtfully. "All of it?"

"Yes. Her good things are here. The cheerleading costume and all."

49

"Well . . . we'll hold onto it anyway, just in case later . . ."

I nodded, watched her leave, and closed the door. Then I nudged the box of locker things into the closet. What would we do with them? What would we do with all of Diane's things?

I went upstairs, used the bathroom, pulled off my white ruffled T-top and dropped it onto my bed. I shifted around in the closet, looking for something cool to wear, like a halter. But Diane and I had put our summer-light things away during a few brief chilly days, and now the closet was crowded with heavy fall and winter clothes.

I looked at the ones that were Diane's. They were just as she left them, some on hangers, some pants and sweaters halfway folded on the shelves, a couple of things kicked into the corner.

There was one special sweater, cocoa-colored with a diamond design of a deeper brown. Made of cashmere, it was a gift to Diane from her adoring mother, Margo. I held it to my face. It felt soft as a kitten.

Diane never wore this sweater. She thought it was good-looking, but "The color's not all that great for me," she said once, when she briefly took it off its padded hanger. "It would look better on you."

"I'll wear it," I generously offered. "Just say when."

Diane and I traded clothes sometimes but we never wore anything until the owner herself had worn it at least once. "Breaking it in," we used to call it.

Diane had never broken in this sweater and I wondered if I'd ever dare wear it. The idea of it made me uncomfortable.

50

I put the sweater back into the closet and reminded myself to ask Mother what we were going to do with Diane's clothes.

And then it came back to me, the sickening scene when Margo was here in this room, the day after the suicide. She was going through Diane's things to choose what she would wear in the coffin.

I happened to be in the room myself, lying down with a cold cloth on my eyes. I had a sinus headache. I took the cloth away and rose when Mom and Dad and Margo came into the room. Margo strode over to the closet and opened the door as though she did this every day.

"These are Diane's things?" she asked.

"Yes, to the right." I sat there, one leg under me, the other braced on the floor.

Mom moved to me and put a hand on my shoulder. She looked washed out. So did Dad. Margo was white-faced, but grim and determined.

"Look, Margo, do we have to . . ." Dad was rubbing his palms up and down the side of his pants. I'd never seen him so physically nervous.

"Robert," Margo said, looking squarely at him, "as disagreeable as this is, it must be done. And I want your opinion."

"Just go ahead," he said. "Pick something. Anything."

"Now listen, I'm not going to make this decision on my own and then someday have you criticize. . . ."

"Damn it, Margo! Do you have to make a scene, now of all times?"

Mom moved to Dad, touched his shoulder, and

then went over to Margo. "I think there are a couple of dresses . . . there toward the end, in back of the tops. . . ."

Margo shoved clothes on hangers to the left, lunged deep to the end for the dresses, and dragged them out. One, the yellow, was still in its transparent dry cleaner's bag.

"Hmmm." Frowning, Margo held one in front of her, and then the other. "What do you think, Robert, the blue or the yellow?"

He took a breath. "Does it make a difference?"

"Well, yes it does. I want her to look nice."

"Nice?" Dad said heavily. "Nice? Margo, Diane is dead. She's going to look dead no matter what she wears."

"She always liked the yellow," Mom said, glancing at me. I knew she meant I should keep out of this and not offer any opinion. We both knew Margo had given Diane the yellow dress.

"Yes, well." Margo still couldn't decide. "You know what?" she said suddenly, folding both dresses over her arm. "Maybe she should wear her cheerleading outfit. She always looked so cute in it."

"Margo, that's the most outrageous thing you've said yet!" Dad looked ready to hit her. "What's with you, anyway! Don't you realize that Diane is . . . ! Cheerleading!" He was almost out of control, pacing now, fists clenched, face fiery red.

"C'mon, Dad," I said, scooting over and taking him by the arm. "Let's go downstairs, find Nell and Ned, see what they're up to." It had slipped my mind that they were gone, but that was all right. It got Dad out of danger . . . the danger that he might go over the edge.

"She was my baby, too!" Margo shouted after us. "Don't think you're the only one . . . !" I could hear her sobbing as Dad and I went down the stairs, and Mom trying to comfort her.

I remembered all this as I gazed at Diane's clothes quietly waiting in the closet. Eventually they'll be taken away. Bit by bit the things that were hers will go.

I stretched out my arms and wrapped them around a bunch of the hangered skirts, tops, dresses. I buried my face in the fabrics. Diane, oh Diane. Diane . . . Diane . . .

6

I get the feeling now and then that the bad times are in the past. My life, I think, is getting back in balance. And that's when something pretty awful suddenly happens.

Today started out well. I went to art class and handed in the pencil drawings that were overdue. Mrs. Cameron had been understanding when I told her they'd be late, and she was complimentary as she sifted through them.

"Bethany, these are really nice. I like them. I especially like the one of the little boy. It looks natural and unposed."

"Well, he was watching TV and forgot I was drawing him."

In any case, Ned's expressions never change a lot. He gives a little crooked smile now and then, but mostly he's solemn.

I tried to do Nell when she was sitting beside Mom, listening to one of her storybooks. But she kept glancing up at me, and every once in a while she'd scoot over to check out what I was doing.

"Nell, if you can't sit still," Mom finally said, "I'll just wait and read to you another time."

"No!" Nell protested. "Now!"

"I'll do this later," I said, getting up, and thought, *when she's asleep.*

I went into Nell's room that night and by the light of the Little Bo-Peep lamp did a quick sketch of her, and thought it was pretty good until I studied it in my room. Then, something about the way she was lying there, eyes closed—

I tore it up. I retrieved the earlier one I'd done of her, the one the girls had seen that day, and added a little more detail from memory. The teacher wasn't going to know how much the drawing resembled the subject. All she really cared about anyway was technique.

Other kids were coming into the art studio, drifting to their easels, checking out supplies. Julie wandered in and stretched to look at my drawings, over the teacher's shoulder.

She followed me to my work area. "I guess you decided not to hand in the one of Diane?" she half-whispered.

I shrugged and fingered the pencils, looking for the ebony with soft lead.

"Right," Julie murmured, and walked over to her own easel.

Actually, Julie and Rebecca and Andrea buffered me from kids who might ask questions, especially in the more informal classes like this art session, or during gym or ballet. At lunch hour the four of us have a place staked out at the end of a table. We might as well have put up a KEEP AWAY sign because kids got the message in the form of hostile stares from Julie and Rebecca especially.

But still, I feel watched. Just yesterday, the girls and I were laughing over some little thing. I happened to glance down the table and saw Cissy Monroe checking me out. I looked away. When I looked back, she was buzzing at some girl next to her and then they both gave me a look. It made me feel guilty. *How could I laugh, when . . . ?*

School was out and I was hurrying down the hall when I heard my name called. I turned to see Ms. Morris, the Spanish Club teacher. She's tiny and snappy-looking, and wears her dark full hair pulled to the side and held with a red and gold comb. I think she's trying to give the impression that she's really Spanish. Maybe she is.

"Are you sure you can't make it to the meeting?" she said, laying a hand on my arm. "We do need you. You're our secretary."

"I know, but Bette said she'd take notes for me. Anyway, I guess I'll have to drop out."

"Oh, don't say that." She steered me away from the flow of kids in the middle of the corridor, and over to the wall. In a lowered, sympathetic tone, the kind people seemed to assume these days, she said, "Bethany, I know it's difficult for you to enter into activities again, but dear, you must do it. It does no good to shut yourself away, to grieve in solitude. I know, because I went through the same thing myself, when my mother died."

You didn't go through the same thing, I wanted to protest. *Your sister didn't commit suicide. Your mother probably died after a long illness.* But I said, "I know what you mean, but it's just that I *can't* stay after school now. I have to go home and take care of my little sister and brother."

Ms. Morris looked distressed.

"So you'd better get some girl to take my place as secretary."

"Or boy," Ms. Morris said almost automatically. She's a great feminist.

"Right." There were only three guys in the club and they were all duds. "Well, I've got to get going."

"Yes, Bethany." And she slipped into the Spanish mode with, *"Buenas tardes, señorita."*

"Adios." I didn't add señora or señorita because with the Ms. in front of her name I didn't know if the teacher was married or not.

Nell and Ned weren't home yet so I took advantage of the time by dialing Andrea.

"Hey," she said. "I was about to call you. Want to come over Saturday afternoon? We're going to make taffy apples."

"Who's *we?*"

"Rebecca and Julie. Maybe Shelley, if she can get out of going to the mall with her mother."

"No guys?" I said it just to say something.

"You never know. Actually, Chris and some guys might stop by. *Might.*"

57

"Whoa. You mean I might get to meet him? *In person?*" Andrea talked about Chris every once in a while. They'd worked on a play together, back in the suburb where she used to live. To hear her tell it, this guy was cuter than any of the hunks we saw in movies. "Does Chris drive now?"

"Not yet. He can't even take driver's ed until next spring. His brother Hank may drop him off. But I don't know. Chris says whenever he comes over his brother teases him so much it's hardly worth it."

"Really, he said that? It's hardly worth it?"

"Well, you know," Andrea said. "Why is it supposed to be so funny when someone under sixteen likes someone else, but after that, it's okay?"

"Don't ask me why. Of course, I don't have a boyfriend."

"What about Kevin?"

"Kevin? Come on."

We talked for about ten more minutes and then I happened to glance at my watch. It was three thirty. "Andrea, I'd better check out the kids," I said.

"Okay. Try to come over Saturday. It'll do . . ." She stopped. "It'll be fun."

As I hung up I knew what Andrea had been about to say: *It'll do you good.* People keep saying that to Mom and Dad and me, and I know they mean well, but it's annoying all the same. How do they know it . . . whatever it is . . . will do us good?

I went to the hallway outside my room but couldn't hear anything. Surely Nell and Ned were home by now. I called downstairs. No answer.

I clattered down the stairs and saw the front door was partly ajar. Some fall leaves had drifted in between the storm door and the regular door. I picked up one that had come in on the carpet and let it flutter out the door.

Where were the kids?

I went to the kitchen. The lid from the teddy bear cookie jar was off. So they were here, or at least had been here.

I looked out the windows toward the backyard. The bushes along our property had turned a greenish yellow, and the yard was full of leaves from the giant oak. Someone ought to rake them up. I'd heard somewhere that oak leaves can kill grass. The grass was a little high and looked damp. I wondered if Dad would mow it once more or just leave it until next spring. Well—there were more important things than grass.

Ned's football, looking a bit flat, was lying on the edge of the patio. No one had put plastic over the redwood furniture out there. There was still time, but we probably wouldn't use it anymore this year. And who cared, anyway.

Where were those kids?

Had they taken off for some friend's house? They weren't supposed to do that without asking first.

I roamed through the house, doubting that they'd be hiding. I mean, we weren't exactly playful these days. Yet, I looked in every closet, every nook downstairs, and began saying, "All right, monsters. I know you're here. So enjoy yourselves, I'm leaving." I listened, but no scuffling little sounds. Nell, at least, would twitch around and give herself away. But the silence was deadening.

Getting concerned now, I rushed upstairs and at Nell's room flung open the door. The room was ominously quiet and undisturbed. I looked under the bed and in the closet, knowing I'd find nothing.

I dashed to Ned's room and opened the door so hard it hit the wall.

Ned was sitting in his beanbag chair. He looked up from his dinosaur book with no expression, in spite of my sudden, noisy entrance.

"Where's Nell?"

He finished looking at me and then deliberately returned his gaze to the book. He turned a page.

"Ned!" I streaked over to him. "I am talking to you. Would you please answer!"

He turned another page. "I don't know where she is."

I yanked the book from his hands. "What do you mean, you don't know where she is! Did she come home with you?"

"Yes." He wouldn't look at me.

"Okay. Nell came home with you. Did she come into the house?"

"Yes."

"Did she come upstairs?"

"I don't know." He made a grab for the book. I held it behind me. "Did she get a cookie?"

"I don't know."

"Did you get a cookie?"

"Give me back my book." He was holding his

mouth tightly together now, and blinking. Something about his expression moved me.

I stooped at his side. "Ned, honey, I don't mean to ride you, but I'm worried about Nell. If you know where she is, please tell me."

"I don't know." He was pressing his lips harder now, struggling to keep away the tears.

I leaned over to hold him, but he struck out at me. "Leave me alone! Just leave me alone!"

"Ned," I said, getting up, "later on, maybe we could have a game of chess? After I locate Nell?" I tried to sound detached. "You know, it's been a long time since . . ."

He looked away. Wow. He was being a hard case.

"Okay, I guess I'll keep looking, but I have no idea where that kid could be. I'm a little worried." I handed Ned back his book.

When I reached the door he mumbled, looking at his dinosaurs, "She might have went downstairs."

"Gone," I automatically corrected. "Downstairs, you mean, or the basement?"

"Basement."

Why, I wondered, as I clattered down the stairs, would Nell sneak off to the basement? And then it came to me. Of course. With the coast clear, she'd gone down to play with the computer in Dad's office, an activity strictly forbidden. Once, she'd messed up several pages of a report and I thought the punishment from that should have taught her a lesson. This time, I supposed I'd be blamed, too.

The basement door was open and I could see a faint light down there. I didn't turn on the switch to the main light because I wanted to slip up and catch Nell in the act.

I tiptoed down the stairs, went over to the office door, and flung it open, ready to shake and break. But Nell wasn't there.

"Nell?" My voice was tremulous, faint. Where *was* she?

And then . . . I know this sounds crazy, but I actually felt what I'd often read, how the hair on the back of your neck seems to stand up. I mean, I felt spooked, and without thinking about it, I took a step or two backward and then looked out into the regular part of the basement. The light from the computer room sent out a faint glow . . . just enough to pick out from the shadows her form . . . and I yelled with fright.

Nell was lying on the couch. She was lying on the death couch, just as Diane had lain almost two weeks ago. Her eyes were closed and *her thumb was in her mouth!*

I held onto the doorjamb and looked, and took deep, gasping breaths. I couldn't move. I just stood there, hyperventilating, my nails digging into the wooden doorframe.

The basement light flashed on. The whole area was now brightly lit. I tried to move, but couldn't.

Ned came creeping down the stairs. "What's the matter?" he nervously asked.

I couldn't reply. I just stared at the form on the couch.

Ned saw her then. He edged toward her. "Nell . . . ?"

The thumb slid wetly out of her mouth. She opened

her eyes wide. They were the same Renoir blue as always, moist, not glassy.

"Wh . . . what are you doing?" Ned stammered.

"I'm Diane. I'm going to heaven."

With a howling sound, I swooped down and yanked Nell off the couch. Wide-eyed, startled for a second, she then began wailing.

I was crying and yelling. "She's dead, Diane's dead! Don't you understand that?" And Nell was screaming and Ned was shouting, "Don't do that, Bethany!" And I realized I was shaking Nell like a rag doll.

I stopped and sank onto the floor, pulling Nell down with me, holding her against my shoulder. I began murmuring, "There, there, Nell, it's all right. Don't cry, sweetheart, I'm sorry."

"No you're not!" Ned's face, as I looked up, was red with outrage. "You're just mean!"

"Oh, Ned . . ." I reached for his hand, but he dodged, grabbed Nell by the arm, and pulled her away from me, toward the stairs.

They were partway up when Nell stopped, turned and said, "You *are* mean, Bethany! And we hate you very much!"

The words struck me like a giant wave. I sat there on the floor feeling stunned, awash, weak. I put my crossed arms over my knees and bent my head to them. Oh God, I couldn't take this. I really couldn't.

I was so alone. No one really knew how I felt. I was battered, bruised. I wanted to roll into a ball, pull a cover over me, and shut out the world. But I couldn't.

I'd better go upstairs. With a sigh I slowly got to my feet.

I felt a leg muscle twitch. I paused for a moment and my glance fell onto the horrible brown couch. I could see Nell lying there, innocent, pretending. And see Diane, lying there in death, not pretending.

A dread feeling came over me. *Nell.* Was she setting up Diane as a hero? No, she couldn't! I know what kids did when they admired someone very much. They tried to be just like them.

7

W hen Mom got home a while later she could tell right away that something was wrong.

Nell was hunched up at one end of the sofa and Ned at the other. The TV was on, but they weren't watching.

"So?" Mom said. "Don't I rate hugs today?"

The kids looked at her, then me, then nowhere in particular.

"All right." Mom put down her purse. "What's going on?"

"Nothing," Ned mumbled. Nell put her thumb in her mouth, then quickly took it out and wiped it on the tail of her T-shirt.

"I got a little scared and yelled at Nell," I said.

"You shook her. Hard." Ned stared straight ahead.

"I overreacted. I'm sorry." And with my back to the kids, I made a little eye motion upstairs that let Mom know I wanted to tell her something in private.

Mom picked up her purse. "You guys should go outside for a while. Take advantage of this nice weather. It's going to turn cold any day now." She waited. "Go on, scoot."

Reluctantly the kids got up and dragged toward the kitchen.

"Put on your jackets if you go out," Mom called after them. "You could rake a few leaves." When they got out of hearing she said, "Good luck to *that* idea."

She flicked off the TV, headed for the stairway, and I followed. In her room, certain that the kids couldn't hear, she said, "What exactly happened, Beth?"

"I couldn't find Nell and finally I went downstairs to the basement and there she was."

"Playing with the computer."

"Playing dead."

Mom turned sharply. "Playing *what?*"

"She was lying on the couch, just the way Diane was. With her thumb in her mouth. I nearly freaked out."

"You're sure she wasn't just napping?" Mom said uncertainly.

"No way. She even said she was Diane and was going to heaven."

"Oh my God." Mom sank to the edge of the bed.

"And it shook me up so much that I . . . I shook *her.*" I stood there clenching my hands, feeling weepy, ashamed, confused. "Mom, I don't think Nell understands! Shouldn't someone explain things to her?"

"How can you explain?" Mom looked so tired. A blue vein by her temple was throbbing. "I think it's better left alone. The least said, the better."

"I don't agree. But that's not the only thing I'm worried about."

66

Mom heaved a big sigh and gave me a resigned look. "All right, let's hear it. What else?"

"I'm afraid Nell may be imitating Diane. Not just like she did today, but in other ways."

"Bethany." Mom shook her head, sighed again, and as she wearily leaned over to take off her shoes, said, "Nell adored Diane. You know that. It was a case of opposites attracting. Healthy, dark-haired big sister, delicate blond little sister . . ."

"Mom, you're being so . . . !"

"So *what?*" She straightened and gave me a steady look. "I'm being *what?*"

"So ununderstanding! Haven't you seen how Nell's beginning to throw a tantrum when the least little thing . . ." I paused.

"Go on, say what you want to say."

"She has no patience. She wants what she wants *right now.*"

"Anything else?"

"There are other things. I just can't think of them with you looking at me like that."

"Fine," Mom said, getting up and putting her white nurse's shoes in the closet. "You've told me now. But the things you've complained about are fairly average for a high-spirited child Nell's age. I agree she's upset, but then we're all upset. You're upset." She came over and put her hands on my shoulders. "It doesn't help to pick at each other, Beth." She looked at me with sad, sad eyes. "Can't you understand that?"

My throat became one big lump. I pulled away from Mom and left the room. What was the matter with this family anyway? My God, Mom, who'd always been so clearheaded was like an ostrich now, with her head in the sand. Didn't she get it? Couldn't she see that Nell's little fantasy held some kind of danger? It scared me. How could Mom brush it aside?

In my room I knew I could easily give in to dread, depression, fear, and exhaustion. I had before. It was horrible. Diane, who used to fling out the words, "I can't help it, I'm depressed!" had probably never known this kind of depression. I couldn't give in to it again. I could, but I wouldn't. I dragged out my math book, depressing in its own way, but solvable. After a while I lost myself in the neat problems on the page and by the time I went downstairs my mood had lifted.

It looked as though everyone else's had, as well.

Mom had let Nell bake biscuits for dinner, the kind you peel from a cardboard tube and are practically foolproof. Nell was delighted. Her eyes and mouth rounded with awe when the toasty brown biscuits came out of the oven. "I did it!" she squealed. And she turned her little face up to me and smiled with pure love.

"They're gorgeous," I told her. "Nell, you're a born cook."

Mom smiled at me. I smiled back.

Dad came home with some new dinosaur stickers he'd managed to find for Ned. Ned raced with them up to his room and had to be called a couple of times when we were ready to eat.

Dinner went off well, almost naturally, for the first time since it happened. Maybe we had turned a mental corner. Maybe we were on the mend. I began to think that the folks might possibly be right. Distract the kids, keep them busy, go on with the daily routine. I noticed that it was beginning to feel natural, having just five places at the table. In time we might begin to forget.

Up in my room, though, there were too many reminders of Diane to let me forget even for a minute. Everywhere I looked . . . memories.

Above her bed was the poster she'd gotten at a rock concert last year with Steve, and I recalled how the folks hadn't wanted her to go, but finally gave in. Her pink cube clock radio next to her bed still ticked away the hours. I'd silenced the radio alarm the first day and never set it since. I knew her cassette player and headphones were in the drawer of the table. I'd picked them up from the floor and put them there myself.

For a moment I imagined Diane lying on the couch in the basement with the earphones. She almost always fell asleep wearing them. But on that Friday she'd had something more serious on her mind. More deadly. What had she thought about before the pills took hold and carried her away? What could she have been thinking about?

Absently, I wandered to the white shelves built against one wall and picked up the teddy bear wearing a tux. Who'd given it to her? Steve? Oh, no, it was her mother . . . Margo . . . given in honor of Diane's first . . . and last . . . prom. The holiday prom last year, Diane wearing red.

And the fairy dancer in the glass globe. I put back the bear and picked up the little musical toy, a gift from Diane's grandmother several years ago. I turned the key and the fairy, wand in hand, turned to the tune of "When You Wish Upon a Star."

I jumped, hearing Dad's voice behind me. "Diane had that a long time." I hadn't heard him come into the room.

"Diane loved it." We listened until the dancer and music wound down, then I put it back. I almost asked what we should do with Diane's things but somehow I didn't want to have that conversation right now.

"I just came to tell you"—Dad looked at the open doorway and lowered his voice—"that I'm having my friend Bob pick up that couch in the basement on Saturday. Will you be here?"

"I was thinking of going to Andrea's, but . . ."

"Well, you go ahead. I'll give Bob the key in case no one's here. In fact, I'll be sure to ask your mother to get the kids out of the house."

"I'm sorry about Nell, Dad. I guess Mom told you what happened."

"Yes, and I blame myself for not getting rid of that thing right away." He shook his head. "To think of her lying there. . . ."

I thought he meant Nell lying there, but then he said, "Dead. All alone, down there in the basement." He had a catch in his voice. Then he glanced around the room and said, "Let's get rid of all the reminders, huh, Beth? And then maybe we can . . ." Without finishing the sentence, he bent his head and left the room.

I finished the sentence for him. *And then maybe we can begin to forget about Diane. Her death.*

But was that what we wanted to do? What we ought

70

to be doing? Forget Diane? How could we forget Diane?

I closed my door, turned out the lights.

I sat in the rocker Diane used to sit in when she was in a quiet, dreamy mood. I sat in it the way she used to . . . arms along the arms of the chair, feet tucked up on the seat, crossed Indian-style.

Diane, I thought, *no matter what the rest of the family does, I won't abandon you. I know it's maybe for the best, but I just can't do it. I can't wrap my memories of you in tissue paper and put them in a box. Your going was much too sudden, Diane. I can't say good-bye to you yet. I have to know and understand. I have to try to reason it out, why you put yourself out of this life, what exactly made you do it. If ever I can understand, then maybe I can let you go. But not until then. No. Not until then.*

On Saturday over at Andrea's I had to ring the bell twice before she came to the door, and then she was laughing, and calling out, "We may have to start all over!"

"What's going on?" I went inside and peeled off my sweatshirt.

"Those illiterates misread the directions and the taffy's so hard you could skate on it. What took you so long to get here?"

"Just stuff at home."

As we got to the kitchen, Rebecca was holding the pan by the handle and Julie was digging at it with a wooden spoon. "It's impossible!" she said in her squeaky voice. "Hi, Bethie, look at this mess!"

71

"Boy, you really did it," I said. "What happened?"

"She said to cook it thirty minutes. . . ."

"I did not, I said ten!" Julie gave another jab with the spoon and the pan went flying out of Rebecca's hand and bounced on the floor.

Andrea shrugged. "At least it didn't spill. Let's ditch this loser project and do something real."

"What about all this stuff?" Julie wanted to know.

"I'll put it away." Andrea shoved the package of brown sugar and other things into the cupboard.

"What about the pan?" Rebecca said. "We'll never get this mixture out without an electric drill. Or dynamite."

"Just throw it away," Andrea said, wiping a sticky glob off the counter.

I guess we were all a little taken aback.

"Won't your mother notice?" Julie asked.

"Probably not. She hardly cooks anyway, except in the microwave."

"Even so, my mother would kill me if I ruined one of her pans," Julie went on. "If I didn't kill myself first."

I gasped as the words stabbed me. It felt like an icicle had plunged into my chest.

Andrea and Rebecca looked shocked and a second later Julie realized what she'd said. From her frozen look I could almost tell she was caught between, *Shall I apologize or would it be better to pretend I don't know what I said?*

Andrea recovered first. She snatched the pan out of Julie's hand and tossed it into a plastic bag with some other garbage. "So much for all that," she said in a chipper kind of way. "You guys want to go outside and shoot some baskets, or what?"

It was a strange suggestion, because not one of us was the least bit athletic. In fact, the hoop was on the garage when Andrea moved in and I wasn't sure there was a basketball to go with it.

"I really ought to go," Rebecca said. "I've got some stuff I have to do at home."

"Oh me, too!" Julie said, obviously fibbing, but who cared?

After they left, Andrea and I wandered into the den and flopped down on leather-looking chairs. "I'm sorry that happened," she said. She put her right foot over the opposite knee and bent to examine the sole of her sneakers. "Look at that. A glob of that caramel gook wedged right between these ridges."

She rubbed at it and I could see strands of the sticky stuff rising with her fingers. She took off the shoe and tossed it toward the kitchen. "People say things like that all the time, though. *'I'll die if this happens.'* You just don't notice it until it means something."

"I know. I felt sorry for Julie, she looked so embarrassed. Do you suppose that's why they really left?"

"Could be. I'm sorry she said that and made you feel bad, but I'm kind of glad they did get out of here." Andrea pulled off the other shoe and sent it toward its mate. It landed with a *clunk.*

"Don't you like them? I know Julie's close to being an airhead but she's fun. And Rebecca's okay. I thought they were your friends."

"They are. I'm just relieved they won't be around when Chris shows up."

"Chris! Wow! He's really coming over? I get to meet Mister Marvelous?"

"If you're lucky, yeh you do." Andrea flung her leg over the side of the easy chair. "I'm so nervous."

"About what?" She didn't look the least bit nervous.

"About whether he really likes me or not."

"You nit, if he didn't like you, why would he come over?"

"I mean *that* way. Listen, he's talking about having a Halloween party. Want to go? He said I could invite anyone I want."

"Hmmm, sounds good." I really didn't think I was ready to go to a party, but all I said was, "Is it a date thing?"

"Not really. But if it would make you feel better, you could bring Kevin."

"Kevin! You've got to be kidding."

Andrea gave a teasing smile. "I *know* you insist you're just friends, but come on, tell me the truth now. . . ."

I groaned and slid down in my chair. "What do I have to do to convince you?"

"Go out with someone else, I guess."

I kicked off one of my loafers in her direction. "Like who?"

Andrea leaned over, picked up my shoe, and threw it to a far corner. "Like one of the guys Chris hangs out with. Want him to fix you up?"

My heart gave a little lurch but I scowled. "I hate it when people say 'fix you up.'" I went over, got my shoe and shoved my foot back into it. "Have you met any of his friends?" I hoped I sounded casual.

"Not yet. But he talks about a *Harold* who sounds pretty good."

"Harold?"

"They call him Mac. His last name's MacDonald. Interested?"

"No!" And to make it sound as if I really wasn't, I switched subjects. "By the way, did you make the gymnastics squad?"

"Yeh, I made it. Have to go to the gym to practice, though, because we don't have a basement in this house to set up my equipment." She lowered her stockinged feet to the floor. "What kind of soda do you want?"

"Makes no difference. Anything."

Elaine wandered into the room just as Andrea came back with two Sprites. "Where's mine?"

"Get your own, sleaze," Andrea said cheerfully, handing me a bottle.

"Thanks." I watched Elaine shamble off to the kitchen. She's tall and slim and could easily be a model. "Elaine's really pretty," I said. And then I wondered if I should have said it. Andrea is pretty, too, but in a more All-American Olympic Team way.

"Yeh, she's not bad." Andrea called out over her shoulder, "Bring us some chips while you're at it!"

Elaine came back with some Fritos in a bowl and held them out to Andrea. "Here, take it."

Instead, Andrea just grabbed a handful. "How come we're so fancy?"

Elaine made a sighing sound and brought the bowl to me. "She thinks 'fancy' is a dish instead of a bag. How come you hang around such a scuzz?"

"I feel sorry for her." I took a few chips.

Elaine set the bowl down next to Andrea. "Here, so you can pig out," she said. She flopped onto the sofa, crossed an ankle over the opposite knee, and took a swig of Sprite. "So what are you guys doing, holding a postmortem?"

I probably wouldn't have noticed if Andrea hadn't looked shocked and said, "Elaine, that's so crude!"

"Why?" She looked puzzled. "What's wrong with hashing over the game, even if we did lose?"

"Oh." Andrea looked flustered. "Football."

And then they went on talking about our team and their team, both of them covering up, while I tried to put on an interested face. But underneath it all, I knew what I was thinking and so did they.

It was about that word. Postmortem. What they did to people after they died in some unusual way. Like suicide.

In one little hour, in two little ways, the subject of Diane's death had sprung up. The fact that in each case it was innocent and unintentional didn't help. It only showed that there was no escape. The subject was everywhere, lying in wait, ready to spring and wound.

8

I had to get out of there. I was feeling kind of sickish, and the last thing I wanted to do right then was meet Chris and any friends he brought along. To keep Andrea from feeling guilty, I said I'd promised to watch the kids for a couple of hours, while Mom did errands.

Walking home, scuffing through the leaves, I felt chilled in just my sweatshirt. The sun that had been so bright in the afternoon had now disappeared behind low gray clouds that might be fog by morning.

I cut through a little kids' park which usually had lots of preschoolers, watched over by their mothers as they spooned sand around in the sandbox (and out of it) or swooped high in swings.

Today, at least now at four o'clock, there were no little energized bodies bopping around, no high-pitched squeals. The sandbox, a mass of humps and hollows and footprints, was empty except for one small red shovel. The swings hung listless, abandoned. Something about this scene gave me the shivers.

I walked faster, got out of the park, started down our street. I'd always liked autumn, but not this year. I used to feel full of zip and energy after the slow, sluggish summer. But now I felt only the sadness of saying farewell to sunny days.

This weather seemed to make the loss of my sister even harder to bear. But what if she'd died during the summer? If Diane had left us on a bright blue and golden day, wouldn't it have been ironic? Like, how can anyone choose to die when nature is on a high?

Stop depressing yourself, I told myself. Think of something else. Think about the Halloween party that Andrea said Chris was giving. I was almost sure I wouldn't go, but if I did, what would I go as?

I couldn't think of a thing. My mind wouldn't even turn in an inventive direction. Something was blocking my thoughts, pushing me off into another path.

Postmortem. That was the block. Postmortem. What they did to dead bodies.

Some months ago, last spring I guess, several of us were sitting around shooting the breeze and a kid named Jerry said, "Bet you can't guess what I saw on Saturday."

"What?"

"My uncle and I were going to a game, but first he said we had to stop by the morgue in the city."

"The morgue? What for?" we all wanted to know.

"He's a coroner's pathologist, and he had to stop by and sign some papers. So I went in with him. And while I'm standing there, they bring in this stiff on an aluminum cart. And the guy's totally naked except for a tag tied to his toe."

"Oh, gross," one of the girls said.

"You think that's gross? You should hear what they do to him. They slice the guy open right down the middle. And saw the ribs apart."

"I don't believe that," someone said.

"Believe it. But that's just the beginning. They drag out all the organs, the stomach, the liver, the what do you call it . . . pancreas. And they slice off sections and send them to the lab."

"What for?"

"Tests. To find out why the guy croaked."

"That is just so disgusting, Jerry." I guess we all thought it was, yet not one of us walked away.

Now that he had us hooked, Jerry gave a slow smile then said, "And when they've finished with the slicing and dicing, they shove whatever's left over into a plastic bag and stick it back into the cadaver and stitch him back together."

"Come on," one of the guys said, "don't try to tell us you saw all that. Or you'd still be throwing up like crazy."

"I didn't say I *saw* it. I said that's what they do. And if you don't believe me, I'll give you my uncle's number. You can call him up."

Nancy, making a little gagging sound, said to me, "Aren't you glad you're a girl?"

Jerry overheard her. "What difference does that make?"

"Why . . . because that could never happen to us."

With a bit of a sneer, Jerry said, "Oh come on, grow up. It doesn't make one damn bit of difference if the stiff is male or female."

Nancy blushed furiously. And at the time, I guess I was thinking what she was . . . how awful to be wheeled in on a cart . . . *naked!*

Now an entirely different thought took hold of me. Diane! *By law, they do a postmortem in every case of accidental death.*

As the nausea rose in me I tried to stanch it with . . . *but hers wasn't accidental. She did it deliberately.* It was no use. I began retching. I went to a tree, leaned my forehead against it. *They cut her apart, reached in* . . . my stomach heaved and liquids came up and burst from my mouth. I leaned against the tree, gagging over and over until finally the nausea subsided. I tried, in my mind, to blot out the scene in the morgue, to picture instead Diane in her coffin. She lay in her yellow dress, makeup on her lifeless face, her hair a bit too perfect, a yellow rose in her stiff, lifeless hands. A prettified corpse. And beneath all that . . . another heave. But there was nothing more to come up.

I wiped my mouth, took a few deep breaths, hoped no one had been watching from a window. But so what. Who cared? All right, I told myself, you've given in. You've thought the thought, you've seen the scene, you've experienced it all. And now it's over. Whatever was done to Diane is over. And you don't ever have to think about it again.

We had Mexican food for dinner. Usually it's one of my favorites but tonight I had no appetite.

"Something wrong, honey?" Dad asked. "Aren't you feeling well?"

Naturally, I couldn't say why I wasn't eating. "I was over at Andrea's," I said. "I guess I had too much junk food."

Nell fixed me with her portrait eyes. "Junk food is bad for you," she said.

"Eat," Mom told her.

"Do you feel like going over to Aunt Pat's with us?" Dad asked.

"Not really."

"I'll stay home with her," Ned offered, a little too eagerly.

"Never mind," Mom said. "I'm sure she can manage alone."

I could hardly wait until they left, so I'd have the house to myself, do anything I liked. But when I was alone, I couldn't think of anything I really wanted to do.

After a while I slumped in front of the TV and flipped from station to station. It was too early for the Saturday night movie, and nothing good was on. After a while, I just stared at some dumb show with the sound turned down.

Why couldn't I get Diane out of my mind? Was I losing my grip, going over the edge? No. It was because her death was a mystery. I knew the ending, but not the motive.

Why? Why had she done it? Surely someone could provide a clue. But who?

Was it Steve, the old boyfriend Diane had stolen away from Heather?

Was it Max, who had stolen Diane from Steve?

Or Hope, Diane's oldest friend?

I closed my eyes and tried to remember how it had all started with Steve. Last summer . . . last *year,* last summer, Diane had been a lifeguard at the community pool. It was the kind of job Diane liked; she didn't have to do much of anything and she could get a tan at the same time.

As far as I know, she was never called upon to save any lives. The closest she got to action was climbing down from her perch and yelling at kids when blowing the whistle alone wasn't enough.

Sometimes I'd go to the pool with Nell and Ned, neither of whom was crazy about the water. Diane wasn't crazy about having them there, either, because Nell was always trying to hang around her and that blew her hotshot image. So one day I was surprised when Diane motioned me to come over. I mean, she didn't need a mere eighth-grade sister hanging around, either.

She climbed down when I got to the lifeguard station, and with her back to the pool said, "Look over my shoulder, over there on the opposite side, but don't look as though you're looking. Hurry up."

"Hurry up *what?* What am I supposed to be looking at and not looking at?"

"The guy in the blue trunks. With that sleaze job in the yellow tank cut thigh high."

"Yeh. What about her?"

"Not her. Him. Isn't he darling? Beth, don't stare. You're staring."

"I am not. My eyes are stinging. I wish they didn't let so many little kids get in the pool, then they wouldn't have to load it up with so much chlorine."

"Is he looking this way?"

"No. Diane, is that all you wanted?"

"Yes. Why are you so negative?"

I didn't think I was being particularly negative, but I didn't argue, just left. When I got back to the kids I saw Diane standing on the platform now, hands on her hips, slightly up on her toes to make her calves look slimmer. I don't know whether the guy noticed her or not. That day, I mean. It doesn't matter. He did later.

"I found out his name," Diane said suddenly, as we lay in our beds in the dark about a week later. "It's Steve. Isn't that great?"

"That his name is Steve?"

"No, amoeba-brain. That I saw him again. It was just by chance. I was leaving the perch, ready to go off duty, and there he was."

"Doing what?"

"Nothing. Standing there. But he was alone!"

"And he said, 'My darlink! At last ve are alone!' "

"Look, Beth, if you're going to be snide. . . ."

"I'm sorry. What did he really say?"

"He said, 'Do you happen to know if the pool will be open on Labor Day?' "

I paused. "Will it be? Why couldn't he just read the pool notice?"

"You ditz! That's not the point. His being there wasn't accidental. He had deliberately set out to meet me!"

"Wow." To be nice, I asked Diane if he'd said anything else.

Even though she was a little miffed at me, she

couldn't resist going on. "He said his name was Steve. And I told him mine was Diane. And if you think he's cute from a distance, you should see him up close. He's like one of the guys on 'The Young and the Restless.' Muscles. Wow. He must be a weight lifter."

"Did he say anything else?"

"No, the manager called me then, and I had to go into the office. But Steve said he'd see me around."

School started the day after Labor Day. One night, again after lights were out, Diane said, "Guess what. I saw him today in the hall."

Caught up in my own thrills of eighth grade, I mumbled, "Who?"

"That hunk, Steve. The one I told you about at the pool? Only he wasn't alone. That girl was with him. Her name's Heather, and I hear she's his steady."

"Too bad."

"Yeh. For her, when I take him away."

"How can you, if she's his steady?"

"Oh Beth!" I felt, rather than saw, Diane flopping from her back onto her side, slapping down the pillow. "It's so hard to talk to you sometimes. You're so . . . innocent!"

"I'm sorry. How are you going to take him away?"

"It depends. First I'm going to find out as much about this Heather as I can. Then when I know exactly what she's like, I'll be just the opposite. If she's quiet and adoring, I'll be lively and play hard-to-get, and . . ."

"Diane, why don't you just be yourself?"

"That might not do it."

"Sure it would. You've got a lot going for you."

Since she was quiet and I sensed she wanted to hear more, I said, "For one thing, you're healthy-looking."

"Oh please!" she said, really irritated.

I realized that's what Dad always said. "Diane you look wonderful today. So healthy-looking."

"Well, it's a lot better than being pale and skinny like me," I added. "If I could only tan the way you do, instead of getting freckled and sunburned. . . ."

Diane wasn't interested. "We're not talking about tans. We're talking about strategy."

"You make it sound like some stupid political campaign." I reached down and scratched a mosquito bite on my ankle. "You know what Dad says about those guys running for office. . . ."

"Beth, could you possibly stay on the subject?" Diane raised herself up. "What's the matter? What are you doing?"

"I've got some itchy mosquito bites. I guess I'll go rub soap on them." It was an old remedy that usually worked.

When I came back and settled down in bed, Diane said, "Margo has some pretty good ideas about men."

I thought, *I'll bet she has*. Besides being married twice, Margo bragged about having had several affairs.

"She says if a woman spots a man she wants she should make sure he notices her."

"Diane, guys notice you. Remember when Hope said you ought to get a ticket for obstructing traffic? That half the male students hang around your locker?"

"Oh, so what. I want this one special guy. I don't

care about the others. So what I've got to decide is what to do and then wait for the right moment to do it. Steve is the one I absolutely have to get."

There was no use in my commenting that people don't always get what they want. Diane didn't believe it applied to her.

I was yawning into my pillow as her voice said dreamily, "I'll make sure that boy remembers me next time we meet . . . wait and see."

It was only a day or two later that she had that meeting. Diane didn't mess around, once she made up her mind.

Again, I was half asleep when she started in. "I did it. I made Steve notice me."

I mumbled, "Ummm . . . how'd you do that?"

"I saw him coming down the hall, alone, just as I was about to close my locker. So I reached back in for a book I didn't really need, turned suddenly when I felt him near, and then dropped the whole bunch of books."

"You did? Why?"

"Idiot! So he'd stop and help pick them up."

"Oh."

"Beth, are you awake?"

"Yeh, yeh, I'm awake."

"And I managed to stoop toward the same book he was, so we'd bump heads."

This sounded dumb, and yet in a way instructive, as dumb things sometimes are. "What happened next?"

"He gave a little gasp . . . and he reached over and *touched my forehead!*"

"Was there a bump on it or something?"

"Oh, you dense blob!" Diane reached across and whacked me with her pillow. "Why do I bother talking to you?"

"I just want to get it straight in case I need to use the idea. Someday."

Diane went on with her story. "When I had all the books in my arms I looked at him with a tiny frown and said, "It seems to me we met . . . oh I know. At the swimming pool!"

"And he said, with the cutest grin, 'I was hoping you'd remember.' Can you believe it?"

"Wow," I said.

"Yeh, really." I guess Diane was too overcome to say anymore.

I went to sleep.

I don't know if Margo said so or if Diane just knew these things, but the next night she told me it wasn't very smart for a girl to chase after a boy. "Once you get him to notice you," she said, "you act somewhat interested, but you also act very involved with your friends. If he really wants to know you better, he'll do something about it."

She paused. "Why are you making that face?"

"It sounds so phony . . . 'act this way, act that way.' Don't you have any confidence at all?"

"Of course I do. I have confidence that it'll work."

And it seemed to, all right. Diane reported that after a few days of Steve coming down the hall and seeing her surrounded by, and cutting up with, kids, he'd taken her aside and said, "Don't I ever get to see you alone?"

"If that's what you want," she said.

"It's what I want."

And just like that, they started hanging out together. Heather was history.

9

Diane and Steve didn't go out on *date* dates at first, because the folks wouldn't let her. Dad didn't like the idea of Steve being over at the house when no adults were around, either, until he met him. Then Dad said Steve seemed okay. He called him a healthy-looking young man.

Both Steve and Diane were involved in lots of school activities. Besides being a cheerleader, Diane was also on the girls' volleyball team and Steve was into basketball and wrestling, as I've said. The wrestling and working out were probably what gave him the muscles.

Nell and Ned used to love to punch him on the biceps as hard as they could and all he'd do was laugh. Once, Ned punched him in the nose and that wasn't so funny. It gave Steve a nosebleed and Diane was furious at Ned, but she didn't tell Dad.

This all started last fall, a year ago. Diane and Steve became an overnight item. I mean, everyone knew they were crazy about each other. Guys stopped hanging around Diane after Steve threatened to crack a few skulls. The two of them were together as often as they could manage, and if they weren't together, they were linked by phone.

They had almost a computer printout of each other's schedules. If Steve was at practice, Diane worked herself into fits if he didn't call the minute he was finished.

One day after school Diane and I were in our room. When the phone rang, she yelled, "I'll get it!" and did a belly flop on the bed. "Yes, Steve?" And then the tone changed. "Oh, Hope."

I went to the closet to look for an old leotard I kept around for exercise.

"Oh, that's too bad," I heard Diane say, and then, "Hope, could I call you back? I'm waiting for a call from Steve."

I looked over at Diane when she hung up. "What was the matter with Hope?"

"She lost her after-school job. Her boss hired his niece instead."

"Boy, you sure were sympathetic."

Diane flushed and looked irritated. "What am I supposed to do, find her another job?"

I yanked up the leotard. "You could have at least said you were sorry and listened to what she had to say."

"Oh, stuff it," Diane said, getting off the bed. "Besides, she knows I'll call her back after Steve calls."

She stalked toward the bathroom. "We wouldn't have this problem if Dad would just get *call waiting!*"

Diane was really possessive about Steve. One day after school I was out in the kitchen and heard them arguing in the living room.

"So! You admit it! Heather still calls you!" Diane was shouting.

"Once. Just once. If I'd known you were going to make such a big deal of it I wouldn't have said anything. Here I'm trying to be, like, open and honest and you get into this mean mood."

"Oh, sure, it's my fault. How would you like it if some guy *I* used to go with called *me* up?"

"Well, I wouldn't blame *you.*"

"Fine. I may give Paul Sykes a call, then."

"You said if *he* called up. You didn't say if *you* called up."

I turned on the blender to make my health drink, and wondered if love made everyone this stupid. When I switched off the blender it was quiet in the living room. I glanced over at the sofa as I went upstairs and they were all kissy-kissy. "You guys are real mature," I said under my breath, but I don't think they heard me.

Now, sitting alone in the living room, I see that a comedy show has come onto the TV, but I still don't turn up the sound.

I'm trying to think back to when all this changed, this great love connection between Steve and Diane. When was it that Max came onto the scene? Early spring, late spring? I can't remember. I just remember happenings . . . phone calls late at night, Diane slipping out of the house several times after everyone else was asleep, and never getting caught. I didn't ask her where she went or what she did. I didn't want to know.

At about the same time I remembered Dad was having business problems at the insurance office because of new management. Also, Grandma Gwen was in the hospital with a broken hip.

This one Friday night Dad had taken Nell and Ned into the city to visit Grandma because she was finally back home and said she couldn't stand it unless she saw those precious kids right away. Diane wasn't around. Mom was working a rare late shift at the hospital. I had a job babysitting for just a couple of hours.

Anyway, I got home at about nine o'clock. I expected the house to be empty, so I was startled to see Mom sitting in the living room. Just sitting, not doing anything.

"Mom . . . I thought you had to work late," I said. "How come you're home?" She turned to look at me, but said nothing. "Mom?" It was a little eerie. "Mom, is something wrong?"

"There was . . . an emergency."

"At the hospital?" Then, why was she home?

"Here."

"Here?" What could she mean?

Mom took a deep breath. "I might as well tell you. Maybe you know something I should know. Just don't tell your dad."

"Mom, what is it?" I sat on the sofa and leaned toward her chair. "What's happened?"

She looked at me. "Diane took some pills."

"Pills?" I didn't get it. "For a headache?"

"She took an overdose."

I felt a chill in my arms, my chest. "Diane did? Is she . . . is she all right?"

"Oh, yes. She's all right. She's upstairs in bed now."

I glanced toward the stairs. In a lowered tone, I said, "Mom, how did you find out? Who called you?"

"Diane did, herself. She had them page me at the hospital. She said it was an emergency. I was home in five minutes. I must have run every red light for a mile."

"Was she . . . how did she look?"

"Groggy. I made her throw up, and then I poured coffee into her and kept her moving. She came out of it all right. But oh God, what a scare."

"Poor Mom." I went over, and put my arm around her. "It's too bad Dad wasn't here."

"I'm glad he wasn't. And don't you tell him, either."

"Why not, Mom? Don't you think he ought to know? His own daughter tries to . . . !"

"Listen to me, Beth. Dad has enough problems at work without having this laid on him, too. You know how upset he gets when he's worried. He'd probably have it out with Diane and make her worse than ever. The best thing is to just leave it alone, forget it."

"What made her do it, though? She has her dramatic fits, but she's never gone this far . . . taking an overdose. . . ."

"It wasn't all that many pills, as it turned out. She might even have been able to sleep it off." Mom put her hand at the back of her neck and moved her head up and down to relieve tension. "She told me she was depressed." Mom sighed. "That's all. Depressed."

"She didn't say about what?"

"No. Oh, Bethany, what can I do for her? I'm lost. Does she talk to you? What's wrong in her life? When I tried to pin her down she said it was nothing. Nothing. So she takes a few pills." Mom began crying softly. "I love her and I want to help her, but how can I when . . . ?"

I looked over at the clock. "Mom, don't. Dad will be coming home with the kids any minute now, and you know how Ned, especially, seems to pick up feelings right out of the air."

Mom got up. "Will you talk to Diane, Beth? Try to find out what's making her so unhappy?"

"Sure." I gave Mom a hug. "It's probably just something that happened with Steve or . . . someone." I wasn't sure the folks knew about Max. He was a mystery even to me. "Diane probably did it to get attention on a dull evening. You know how she is," I said, trying to lighten Mom up. I started for the stairs, then came back and whispered, "Did you call Margo?"

Mom looked perplexed. "Call Margo? No."

"I guess she'd turn it into a major scene. But . . ."

Mom said, "I'm the one Diane called. I'm the one she asked for help."

"Well, Mom, you're a nurse."

"I know I'm a nurse. But I'd like to think Diane called me because she knows I'm always there for her."

I remember thinking as I went upstairs, *But what if Diane tries it again, and Mom isn't available?*

I blame myself now, sitting in this room six months or so after that night, for not following through on my instincts. For not nagging at Mom to do something . . . tell Dad . . . even Margo, or *someone*. On the way upstairs I had even thought of talking to my junior-high counselor and having her call Diane's counselor. But I didn't.

The reason I didn't, at the time, was it all seemed to be a big fat nothing.

I had gone upstairs with a feeling of dread, expecting to see Diane pale and dragged out, a sopping mess. I opened the door quietly, in case she was asleep. I saw the glow from her bedside lamp and walked in, careful not to make the slightest sound.

Diane was propped up in bed, talking—or rather listening—on the phone. She had a pink ribbon tied around her hair . . . which did look pretty limp . . . and she was wearing a pink nightgown that gave her face a reflected glow. Diane saw me, smiled, and waggled her fingers in greeting.

"Did she!" Diane laughed and said, "What happened next?" And laughed again.

So much for being depressed, I thought. I stood there looking at her, really disgusted. Finally she said on the phone, "Call you back, okay? My sister's here, staring at me." She laughed and said, "Right."

She hung up. "Hi. What's up?"

"Why did you do it?" I said. Anger made my voice crack. "Can you just tell me why you did it?"

"Oh." She looked away. "I guess Mom told you."

When I didn't answer, she said a little sorrowfully, "I guess I was just depressed."

"Oh, how really awful." I couldn't keep a sarcastic tone out of my voice. "What about."

"Just things. You wouldn't understand." She gave a big sigh.

"I have a news bulletin for you, Diane. Everyone gets depressed."

"You don't."

"What!" I couldn't believe she said it. "What do you mean, I don't? Do you think you're just so unique?"

"Well, you don't show it. And if you do, it's not like me."

"True. I don't go swallow pills and call Mom and drive her nearly over the edge." My voice really broke then and I started crying. "You really scared Mom. She doesn't need this kind of grief."

"Oh, Bethy, I'm sorry. It was a mistake. I admit it." Diane twisted some hair around her finger. "It seemed like a good idea at the time, but . . ."

"A mistake! When you could have killed yourself! That's all, just a mistake?"

"Come on." She patted the bed next to her. "Sit down, Bethy. You know I didn't really want to die and be put in the ground. I just kind of wanted to be dead for a little while."

"Oh God." I was crying. "There's no such thing as . . ."

"I'm sorry. I really am." She leaned forward and wiped the tears from my face and put her arms around me. "I'll tell Mom that she doesn't need to worry. I'm all right now. It was just a terrible mood." She turned and sat on the edge of the bed. "Okay?" She kissed my forehead. "Shall we just forget it?"

I nodded. I wanted it to be all over. I wanted to believe it was just a mistake. To be convinced it would never happen again.

And now, months later, here I am alone in the house. Knowing it did happen again. Feeling the guilt. I should have done something. I shouldn't have believed Diane.

But what about Mom? Wasn't she guilty, too? Had she ever told Dad about that night? If she hadn't by now, I hoped he'd never find out. Never.

I kick up the sound on the TV. There's a huge burst of studio laughter. I keep hitting the volume until the laughter crashes against me like a physical force, hurting my ears.

And then I turn off the set. And the silence hurts even more.

10

B ethany, I'm going to need your help," Mom said when I came home a little late one day the next week. I'd been able to stay after school for a Student Council meeting because Mom had taken the day off. From the look of our house, she'd spent the whole time waxing and polishing.

Diane used to say Mom was compulsive about keeping the place clean but at least she wasn't paranoid-perfect like Diane's birth mother.

"You should see Margo's apartment," Diane reported one day. "She redid the decorating and the place is like a showcase, look but don't touch. I made the mistake of actually *sitting* in one of her Italian chairs and she swooped over and said, 'Don't jiggle around, it's not good for the frame. And try not to touch the arms because just ordinary skin oil can stain that fabric.' "

Diane said she had ended up sitting on the floor. Of course, no shoe wearing was allowed.

"And the bathroom . . . it looks gorgeous, all black

fixtures and peach tiles and everything. But every little dab of soap suds shows, every little paw print."

"She has a dog?" The only kind I could picture was a toy poodle.

"No dog. I'm speaking of my own paws. And of course, you'd be struck down by lightning if you dared use those little peach linen hand towels. I just wiped my hands on my T-shirt."

To get back to this day: The house looked fine, so I asked Mom where she needed my help.

"I want you to go through Diane's things with me," she said.

"Oh, Mom."

"I know. But it has to be done." She absently brushed back a lock of hair that had fallen over my eye. "Come on, let's go up and do it."

"Where are the kids?" I asked as we went upstairs.

"Ned's over at Jimmy's. Nell's taking a nap. I'd like to get this over with while they're not around."

She went into my room and I followed, tossing my jacket and brown beret on the bed. There were two empty cardboard boxes on Diane's.

"Oh, Bethy." Mom's eyelids had that pinkish look that showed she'd been crying again. She looked so pale, so weary.

"I know." To keep from weakening, I said, "Where do we start?"

"With the clothes, I guess. You girls traded around so much, I can't tell which are hers and which are yours."

"What'll we do with them? Give them to Margo?"

"No. She told me all she wants are some photographs and a few things she gave to Diane, that's all. No clothes." Mom shook her head and walked to the closet. It was still pretty much of a mess. Sweaters on the shelves may have started out being folded, but now they were every which way. A lot of bulky things were on hooks or kicked onto the closet floor.

"You hand me the things," Mom said, "and I'll fold them and put them in this box."

"Then what will we do with them?"

"I don't know. Give them to Goodwill, I guess."

I started with the easy things . . . clothes that were definitely Diane. Bright colors, shorter skirts than mine. And more jazzy. I kept one skirt that was cut with a flounce and was longer and tighter than Diane's usual things. Besides, she'd turned it over to me.

It was hard to remember which sweaters were whose, especially the older ones. I found one, though, that was really cute . . . red, all wool, with white sheep embroidered on it and just one black one in the flock.

"Remember this?" I asked, holding it up. "Aunt Pat gave it to Diane last Christmas." I could picture Diane wearing it. There was still a faint trace of Diane's cologne. I handed the sweater to Mom.

After a while there were a lot of empty spaces on the shelf and a lot of empty hangers. I took out a bunch of them and shoved them into a garbage bag Mom had brought up for things to be thrown away, like underwear, panty hose, and so on.

The box of clothes was so full Mom couldn't even get the flaps to stay down. "I'll put this in the hall storage closet and then we can get started on the other one."

100

"What's it for?"

"Her other things." Mom left and I looked around. It seemed so heartless to clear every trace of Diane from the room.

"Mom, do we have to do this?" I asked as she came back. "Couldn't we let it go for a while?"

"There's no point in putting it off."

"What about . . . her bed?" I couldn't bear the thought of an empty space where Diane had once lain.

"The bed." Mom's voice faltered, but then she took hold. "The bed can stay. You might want to have friends over. Or maybe even Nell? She might like to sleep in here sometimes."

"Okay. But not for a while. I don't think we should encourage her to . . ."

"To what?" Mom picked up Diane's clock radio.

"I don't know. To try to take Diane's place."

"Now really. Aren't you making too much of Nell's actions? She doesn't know what she's doing. She's just a little girl."

I could have told Mom things I thought about when I was that age, things adults don't realize kids catch onto. I didn't want to get into that, though. Besides, I liked to think I was more sensitive than most kids. "Here's Teddy," I said, handing over the toy.

Mom straightened the tie, looked wistful, then stuck it in the box with a sigh.

As long as we had to do it, I wanted to get it over with, so I just grabbed things and passed them to Mom. I hadn't really realized how many more things Diane had than I. But besides relatives we shared she had others from her mother's side, and they were a bunch of gift-giving junkies.

When Diane's stuff was cleared away I had the feeling that something was missing. Ah . . . the fairy with her magic wand. "I don't see the music box," I said. "That's funny. It was here . . ."

"It'll turn up," Mom said. "What about her sports things in the closet?"

I dragged out skates, a catcher's mitt from several summers ago, stiff and cracked, and a tennis racket and cans of balls.

"Leave the tennis things," Mom said. "Someone can always use them. Maybe Ned, some day."

"Would you want him to have the Sony stuff? It's in the table drawer there."

Mom made a little face. "Not yet. There's plenty of time for Ned to tune in. Anything else?"

"I got rid of her makeup."

"What about the things in the chest of drawers?"

"I'll do it now. Use the garbage bag?"

"Yes."

I helped Mom with the second box and after we'd shoved it into the hall closet she went downstairs and I went back to clear out the chest drawers. We'd each had two, plus a bottom drawer that was a catchall for stuff we didn't want but didn't want to throw away.

I yanked out the third drawer down, Diane's, and got a squeamish feeling, seeing slips, panties, bras, things she'd worn next to her body. I scooped them up and shoved them into the garbage bag.

Her next drawer down had nightgowns and the long T-tops she sometimes wore to bed. There was a bright blue one with the slogan, "It's Better in the Bahamas." Margo had bought that when she'd gone off on a trip to the Islands.

Diane's favorite shirt was a pink one that said, "Squint when you approach, lest my beauty blind you." Steve had brought that one back from some town where the team'd had a wrestling meet. I wondered if Steve would want it back. I decided not to ask.

The only thing left in the drawer was a safety pin. Absently, I closed it and then tossed it into the wastebasket.

What about the bottom drawer? Oh, why bother, I thought. Some day I'd just dump everything out and use the space for storage. But then I decided I might as well do it now, make a clean sweep.

I knelt on the floor and tugged at the handles. The drawer stuck slightly, but I maneuvered it open. As I thought, it held nothing but junk. There was an old swimsuit of mine. Had I really thought I'd wear it again? I threw it out along with a pair of jeans that was ripped and had white paint splotches, a tin ashtray advertising beer, noisemakers from a New Year's Eve party, a once-white tennis cap. Out, all of it.

The last thing was an old flannel shirt, also paint-splotched. I picked it up. There was something beneath it. A crazy instinct told me to leave it alone, not to look under the shirt. But I did. And I saw what the shirt had concealed . . . some sheets of paper towel, splotched with brown.

Brown . . . but somehow, shuddering, I knew. This had once been bright red blood! When I moved the towels, gingerly, by one corner, I saw what they had concealed, and I didn't understand it at all. There was Steve's photo, the eight by ten he'd given Diane some time ago. The glass was smashed. There was one big fragment missing.

Then as I knelt there, trembling, wondering what all this was about, I heard it . . . and believed I was going out of my mind.

How could I be hearing the fairy doll music? But I was. I was. And those tinkling little notes were coming from somewhere right in this room!

11

I crouched there for a few frozen moments, and then some kind of sense returned. I wasn't spacey, I was really hearing it. And the sound, I realized finally, was coming from under Diane's bed.

I slammed the drawer shut, turned, and crawled over and lifted the bedspread from where it grazed the floor. I saw what I knew by then I would see. Sweet little Nell, big-eyed, clasping the music box.

"Nell, you little beast! What do you think you're doing? Come out of there!"

Nell began her babyish whimper as she scooted slowly out, the windup ornament clutched in her little hand.

"All right!" I said as I grabbed her arm just under her shoulder and dragged her to a sitting position. "I asked you what you think you're doing . . . hiding under the bed?"

"Don't yell at me!" Tears formed in her doll-blue eyes and edged beyond the fringe of lashes onto her cheeks. "Besides . . ."

"Besides what?"

"Diane said I could have it." She clutched the music box to her. It tinkled out a few notes and stopped.

Suddenly I realized I was doing it again . . . yelling at the poor little kid. I relaxed, and in a softer tone said, "When did Diane say you could have it, Nell?" I wondered if it was the day she died, or a week before, which would mean Diane had planned in advance to kill herself. "Nell, when did she say it? Try to remember."

"I don't know." Her lips formed a pout. "I'm not lying."

"I know you're not. I just wish you could tell me when."

My baby sister gave me an appraising look, as though trying to guess which answer I wanted to hear. "One day," she said, deciding to play it safe.

I sighed. Nell was a lost cause. "All right, honey. It's okay."

"Are you mad at me?"

"No. I just don't like your hiding under the bed." And swiftly, I tried to think of what Mom and I had said, words not meant for tender ears. I couldn't remember. Suddenly, feeling remorseful, I pulled Nell close to me. The poor little thing couldn't help being confused and lonely, with all the adults around her saying and doing things she couldn't understand. I should spend more time with her, romp a bit with her the way Diane used to.

"What were you doing just now?" Nell asked innocently.

I darted a swift look over my shoulder. Thank goodness I'd slammed that drawer shut before crawling over to the bed.

"I was just cleaning out some drawers. Why?"

"You made a funny sound."

I must have gasped when I saw the blood and everything. Quickly, I said, "Nell, I always make funny sounds, like . . . *meow* . . . *arf arf* . . . *moo moo* . . . ,*"* and I began tickling her. After I saw she was totally distracted, I got up and pulled her to her feet. "Let's go downstairs now. Bring the fairy box if you want to."

"Is this someday?"

"What do you mean, Nell?"

"Diane told me, 'Someday you can have the fairy box.'"

"Oh. Yes, I guess it's that day all right." With her tiny hand in mine we started out.

Halfway down the stairs she stopped and said, "I won't tell."

I stiffened. Oh, no. Had she peeked out from under the bed and seen it? "You won't tell what?" I asked.

"About what's in the drawer." She looked up at me with the look of a small conspirator.

I couldn't possibly ask this little kid not to tell. But it was too bad that Mom and Dad had to know. If I could just have kept the mess to myself and thought about it, maybe asked a few questions, it's possible I could find out what it meant . . . that photo with the smashed glass and the bloody paper towels.

We went on down the stairs. "Mommy's right," Nell said.

"About what?"

Nell sighed dramatically. "You know."

"No, I don't."

"About Ned. She said that Ned didn't know how to tune in to that cassette Sony in the drawer."

The Sony player in the drawer! That's what Nell was talking about. What a relief.

Later on, when the coast was clear, I got a small plastic bag, sneaked upstairs, and put the stained towels and the photo with its smashed glass into it. I hid the bag at the far end of the closet shelf, under a navy sweatshirt.

I felt sure the towels and photo had some meaning. Well, of course they did, or Diane wouldn't have saved them. But what was the meaning? How could I find out?

Okay. I sat in the rocking chair, the thinking chair.

Steve might know. It was his photo.

Max? Maybe he'd smashed the glass over Steve's picture. Why, though?

Hope. Diane told Hope, her longtime friend, things she never told anyone else. While I was almost sure Hope hadn't known in advance about the suicide, she might know some things she'd be willing to tell me now. It was worth a try.

I called Hope and asked if we could meet somewhere, in private. She said I could come by the health store where she was working on Saturday during her lunch hour. "We can go over to the park," she said.

It must be true that opposites attract, or it would be hard to explain why those two girls got along so well. Where Diane looked rosy and robust (or healthy, as

Dad would say) Hope was pale and delicate. Diane's sassy brown eyes had a kind of *Sure, you like me!* look, while Hope's pale eyes had an *I don't expect you to understand me* expression. Diane's brown hair sent out sparks. Hope's was long and straight and oatmeal-colored.

Hope had a quiet dignity, though, and a calm quality that made her a friend Diane could count on. I had a feeling she could help me now.

It was raining on Saturday so instead of going to the park, Hope and I sat in one of the far booths at the health food and restaurant place. Hope brought along a pot of herbal tea and I carried the little floral cups and saucers.

"Aren't you going to eat?" I asked. "I mean, it's your lunch hour."

"No, I pick around at food all the time," she said. "On my actual lunch hour I walk or read or run some errands." She took a sip of her tea. "So what did you want to ask me about?"

Now that I was here, facing Hope, I felt a bit awkward. A drop of tea was sliding down the side of my cup. I rubbed at it with my thumb. "You'll probably think I'm crazy, but . . ."

"I won't think that."

I pulled the cup a little closer. "I keep thinking about Diane. I tell myself that if I concentrate hard enough maybe I'll be able to figure out . . ."

"Why she did it."

"Yes. That's it."

Hope looked off into the distance. "I've asked

myself that same question. A lot. Wondering if she said or did something I should have noticed. I can't come up with a thing." She looked back at me. "Do you feel somewhat cheated, Bethany?"

"Cheated?" I wasn't sure what she meant.

"Yes. Like someone you care about just isn't there for you anymore. Like that person's been taken out of your life and there's no replacement."

"Oh, yes, I do feel that way." It was good to talk like this. "Sometimes I feel guilty, too, as though I should have known and tried to stop her."

"And mad." Hope looked more sad than angry. "There are days that I really get mad at Diane for doing it."

Wow. I'd experienced all those feelings. It was a relief to know I wasn't alone. Maybe lots of people . . . relatives . . . felt cheated, guilty, and angry.

"Was there something special you wanted to know?" Hope asked. "Not that I can come up with any answers. Diane and I hadn't spent much time together lately."

"Do you think it was because of Max that Diane did it?" I blurted. For a second that missing piece of glass in the photo flashed into my mind. But Diane hadn't been murdered. And she hadn't died from wounds, either.

"Max? I don't think so. I mean, they'd broken up and all, but . . ."

"Diane and Max? When?"

"Some time before school started this fall."

"She didn't tell me that."

110

Hope propped an elbow on the table. Her hand fanned out her hair and the tips of her fingers emerged through the strands. "Maybe she was still trying to get him back. I really don't know."

"Where did this Max come from, anyway? Diane told me about Steve from the very beginning but hardly anything about Max. It was as though she wanted to keep him secret and hidden away."

"Maybe she thought you'd disapprove of him, the way most people did." Hope squinted in thought. "As I remember, he showed up at school last spring. Before that he lived in Chicago. I heard his uncle owns a pawnshop and Max spent a lot of time there. Then a social worker got on his case and Max supposedly moved out here to live with his grandmother."

"What do you mean, *supposedly?*"

"Officially he lived here, but he was back in Chicago half the time. Didn't he ever say anything when he was around your house during the summer?"

"I never met the guy. I *saw* him, but Diane always ran out of the house when he came by and off they'd go. I guess she was afraid Nell or Ned would say something about him to the folks." I added a little sugar to my tea. "He looked somewhat weird, from what I saw of him."

"You mean his clothes?"

"His clothes, yes, and his hair." I thought. "Maybe he couldn't afford haircuts. And all he had was secondhand clothes."

"I don't think that's it. Max wanted to be different. It was his choice to wear those white shirts with the

111

tails hanging out, and loose ties, and that floppy duster coat. I think that was his appeal to Diane. That he was so different from other guys."

"How did they ever get together in the first place?"

Hope gave a short laugh. "I had a front seat for that one. It started one day at lunch. I was sitting across from Diane and she seemed rattled. She'd forget what she was saying, and once or twice she blushed. Finally I asked what was going on with her and she said, 'He keeps staring at me.'

"I turned around to look and there was this new guy, Max, totally ignoring the tray in front of him. He was sitting with his chin propped on his hand, looking at Diane. Well. That went on day after day. That is, whenever Max managed to make it to school, which was usually four days out of five."

"Diane never told me any of this."

"The guy spooked her at first. But then she came to expect it and seemed a little let down on the days he didn't make it to school." Hope half smiled and shook her head. "Max knew the right moves. He got her to notice him, got her really intrigued, then made her anxious when he wasn't around. Then he finally claimed her . . . I mean, no doubt about it, she was his little love-slave. In a manner of speaking."

"What did *you* think of him?"

Hope poured more tea. "I thought he was a bit strange. Well, that's no news. Everyone did. At first I guessed it was just an act. *People think I'm weird, so that's the way I'll behave.* But he genuinely didn't care. That was all right. For him. But I didn't like the way he influenced Diane. He got her not to care what other people thought, either." Hope shifted out of the booth and reached for the teapot. "Let me warm this up."

She came back in just a few minutes. "Sorry. Where were we?"

"Talking about weird Max. Hope, there's something I have to ask you about. It's somewhat sick." And I told her about finding Steve's photo and the blood-spotted paper towels. "Can you make any sense of that?"

"Wait a minute." Hope wrinkled her forehead. "That may be . . ."

"What?"

"I shouldn't be telling you this, but . . ."

"What? Come on, please."

Hope leaned back slightly in the booth. "Right at the start of school this fall, remember we had a couple of really hot days? Well, Diane wore long-sleeved shirts on those days while everyone else was wearing tank tops. Then one day in p.e. I noticed a long red scratch on her forearm and Diane said a cat had scratched her."

"We don't have a cat."

"I know. But someone could have." Hope gave me a look. "I wonder if it was done by a piece of glass, though. It could have been."

"But why?" This was really eerie. "Why would she break the glass on Steve's photo and take out a piece of it and run it down her arm? Enough to make it bleed?"

"But not enough to do any real damage. It didn't go across her wrist. I remember that." Hope circled her palms around the teacup. "She had to be doing it for effect. To make some kind of dramatic statement."

113

That was Diane. Always high on drama. "But who was she trying to scare? Steve or Max?"

Hope shrugged. "It could be either. I guess the only way you're going to find out is to ask them."

I felt jittery. I mean, I'm only a lowly freshman kid, and both those guys are older and with it. At least in some ways. How could I go up and ask them? Maybe I could get Hope to do it.

I swallowed and said, "Hope do you think you . . . ?"

"No way."

"I was just going to ask . . ."

"I know what you were going to ask and the answer is *forget it*. For one thing, they'd never open up to me. My feeling about Steve is that he's a jock-jerk and I consider Max a lost cause. Diane knew I felt that way, and she probably told both of them. You know Diane."

"I thought I did."

"But they'd have a different attitude toward you, as Diane's sister." Hope drank the last of her tea. "Bethany, my advice to you is to look up those two guys and ask them what they know. They owe it to you. You have a right to find out."

She smiled, said, "Good luck," and went back to work.

I slid out of the booth thinking that sure, I might have the right, but that didn't mean it would be easy to approach either one of them. Nothing, though, was easy these days. I would just have to grit my teeth and go do it. That's all. Just go do it.

═══ 12 ═══

I don't feel the need to go out there," I heard Dad say as I was coming out of my room on Sunday. "It's not where she is." They were talking in their bedroom but the door was open and the sounds carried down the hall. "But you go, if you think it'll make you feel better. I can't."

"It seems so . . . I don't know," Mom said. "So like we've abandoned her."

"Diane abandoned us," Dad said. "She left without a word."

"Oh, Bob. Try not to blame her so much."

"Then who should I blame? You, Beth, the kids, her friends, her teachers, who?" Dad charged out of the room. I felt guilty, standing there, but he just looked at me, shook his head, and went down the stairs.

"Mom?" I went to the doorway. "Are you okay?"

"Oh yes. I'll survive." She walked to the closet, pulled out a pair of brown pumps, and stepped into them.

"Where are you going?"

"To the cemetery." She leaned toward the mirror and pulled a comb through her hair.

I went closer. "The cemetery? Why, Mom?"

A quick surge of color slammed into her cheeks. "Oh don't you start now." She dropped the comb and turned to face me. "Someone has to go. We can't just . . . let her lie."

"Mmm." I didn't know what to say. "Want me to go along?"

"Yes, if you don't mind."

I was a bit taken aback. I'd thought she'd say no, but now there was no way to get out of it. "Okay, let me get my jacket."

When we got downstairs, Dad was sitting on the sofa, Nell on his lap, reading the Sunday comics to her.

"Has anyone seen my car keys?" Mom asked.

"On the kitchen counter." Dad glanced at me and went back to the paper.

Nell lunged from his lap and raced toward Mom. "Where are you going? I want to go, too!"

"No, baby, not this time. You stay and keep Daddy company."

Ned came in from the kitchen. He had a milk mustache. "Where are you going?" he echoed.

"Oh, just out," Mom said. "You two stay with your father."

Nell's face puckered up. "But I want to . . . !"

"I'll take you guys somewhere," Dad said. "Maybe we can make a pit stop at Dairy Queen." I don't know what he'd do if they ever closed that place.

116

"Here are the keys," I said to Mom as we went through the kitchen. We left fast.

A while later we were driving along the road next to the cemetery. I felt a lurch in the pit of my stomach. It got worse as we went through the iron gates and wound along the graveled cemetery road. What were we doing here? It was strange, horrible, to think we had a reason for being in this place.

As we pulled to a stop and Mom switched off the ignition, I said, "Oh, do we have to?"

"You can stay in the car if you like," Mom said, getting out.

I got out, slammed the door, and stared at the field of marble monuments, silently marking the places of the dead. The light autumn wind swayed artificial flowers in their hanging baskets and blew fallen leaves over the graves.

I followed Mom as she crossed the gravel road. Before we even got to it, I recognized Diane's . . . place. It was the only one heaped with wreaths and sprays of flowers.

And now my stomach lurchings got serious. The last time we'd been here, all of us had left before they lowered the casket. There had been folding chairs for the family, and green, artificial grass had hidden the mound of waiting earth from the eyes of the mourners.

I hardly remembered the ceremony. There was a sense of people, of prayers, of sobs, and beneath it all the feeling that this could not be real, this could not be happening, this could not be my sister Diane in that gray casket, balanced over the waiting hole.

Now Mom and I grasped each other's hands as we approached the rounded mass that marked Diane. I guess we started crying at about the same time.

Oh God! Was she really under there? Was Diane under the ground? I began to sob and turned to Mother, and we put our arms around each other. We were both crying so hard we were shaking.

Finally, Mom pulled away, opened her purse, took out tissues, and handed a couple to me. Wiping away at our eyes, we looked hazily down at the flowers. They were withered and brown, and lay in matted clumps. Once they had been beautiful, bursting with color and life.

"So many," Mom said. "So many flowers." She stooped down and picked out a white rose that had somehow survived. The ribbon nearest it, rain-streaked now and faded, said, *Dear Granddaughter*.

Oh Diane, I cannot believe you are down there, away from our sight, removed from our life forever. And again, I could almost hear her voice, from that time before. *Bethy, I didn't really want to die and be put in the ground. I just wanted to be dead for a little while.*

Mom gave a huge, shuddering sigh, put her arm around my shoulder and we started toward the car. Then she stopped, pulled away, and went back to the grave. Kneeling, she gently replaced the rose.

I went on to the car, tears streaming again.

Mom came back and got in. She turned on the ignition, then turned it off again, and leaned her arms and head against the steering wheel and sobbed in a way I've never heard her sob before. It was awful. Frightening.

After a while I put my arm around her and said softly, "Mom, let's go."

We didn't talk on the drive home. When we got there, Mom slowed down, looked to make sure that our other car was gone, and then pulled into the garage.

There was a note for me fastened onto the refrigerator with a magnetic four-leaf clover. *Beth . . . Andrea wants you to call her.*

"Is it okay if I ask Andrea to come over?" I asked Mom. Andrea was about the only person I knew who could understand how I felt. "Or would you rather I went to her house?"

"It would be nice to have someone else here when the kids get back," Mom said, getting a drink of water. "I'm going upstairs to lie down for a while."

"Good," I said. She looked really dragged out. I knew I looked a wreck, too. I'd ask Andrea to come over in a half hour, to give me time to shower and wash my hair. I felt I needed to do that, to wash away the traces of . . . of the cemetery experience.

Andrea was full of party news. "Chris just called and told me it's going to be in a barn!" We were sitting on the floor in the living room, next to the fireplace. I'd lighted the last of the quick-light logs. "It belongs to his uncle, only he doesn't use it anymore . . . the barn . . . for animals or hay or whatever they use barns for. Won't that be a great place for a Halloween blast?"

"Well, yeh. I guess."

"It'll be so perfect, with cornstalk things that make

119

such a mess in a house or gym, and eerie stuff sitting around."

"Like what?"

"Oh, dummies, fake ghosts . . . only I guess they'd be floating, not sitting. Chris wants me to go over the day before and help fix it up. Want to come?"

"I don't know."

"Beth . . . are you ticked off at me or something?"

"No. Why would you think that?"

"You seem so . . ." She shrugged. After a moment or two she said softly, "Is it . . . Diane?"

I swallowed. "We . . . Mom and I . . . went out to the cemetery a while ago." I swallowed again. "I knew Diane was there, but when we actually saw her grave it was just awful. I mean, my sister, lying out there all alone." My voice broke.

Andrea stared at the fire. "I know. I wouldn't go for the longest time, but finally the folks more or less dragged me."

"They did? How come?"

"I guess it's because in some ways I wouldn't accept it, about Joe. It didn't seem real. I never did see him after . . . the accident. It was like a horrible dream and underneath, I guess, I had this feeling that he was still just away at school." Her hands moved, pinching at her skirt as she talked. I could tell that she wasn't over her brother's death by a long shot. And I wondered if anyone ever did get over someone young and close dying.

"I wish I'd met him. Your brother must have been a great guy."

"He was wonderful! Joe was the best friend I ever

120

had. When it finally got through to me that he was gone forever it was just awful. I felt cheated out of all the years we could have had together."

Cheated. I felt that, too.

"But I'm over that. I mean, it doesn't do any good to moan and groan over what can't be. So I try to think of the good times we did have, and the things he said to me, and the way he helped me in my life."

"What do you mean?" My first thought was he'd helped her with homework or even with extra money for things. I was glad I didn't say it though.

"Joe taught me to be my own self," Andrea said. "He told me I had my own special qualities and knew how to balance out my life. It was tied up in my mind with gymnastics . . . you know, being in charge of your moves."

"Right."

"But still . . ." Andrea gripped her hands against folds in her skirt and her voice rose. "It isn't fair! It just isn't fair! Why did Joe have to die? He was so good. It isn't fair that he had to leave us . . . to leave life . . . !" She started crying. "It just isn't fair!"

I leaned over and put my arm around her. "Andrea, come on, don't cry. Joe wouldn't want you to . . ."

She turned her head away. "How do you know what he'd want? You never met him."

"Yes, but . . ." Oh God. Now I was crying. "I know. When I think of Diane never coming back . . ."

Andrea pulled away from my arm. "It's not the same."

"What do you mean? They're both . . ."

"But Diane *wanted* to die!"

"Andrea! That doesn't make any difference!"

"Oh, yes, it does. Joe was killed in an accident. Diane deliberately . . ."

I felt stunned, as though something had hit me full force. "Andrea . . ." After a moment or two I got up and went to the far end of the couch and sat down.

A couple of minutes passed. Andrea looked over at me and then away. It was awkward, but I wasn't going to be the first to say anything. I mean, she'd really hurt me.

Finally she got up, mumbled that she had to leave, and took a few steps. Then she stopped. "Where did you put my jacket?"

I was about to say, "It's in the closet," and just let her get it and leave, but something about her tone told me to soften up.

I got the jacket, handed it over, and our looks met. Andrea's face crumpled.

"Oh Bethany, I'm sorry," she said with a little sob. "That was so mean." She held out her arms and so did I. As we hugged she murmured through her tears, "Why do I want to hurt you?"

"Because you're still hurting."

"But that's no excuse. I'm really sorry."

"It's okay."

We pulled apart and went outside.

Andrea wiped the last of the tears away with the back of her hand. "I guess in a way I feel hurt because people . . . I don't mean you, but other kids . . . act as though Joe is a thing of the past. Over and done with, history. It's weird, because I don't want to talk about it myself, but when they just act as though it never happened, I resent that." She managed a crooked smile. "Nuts, huh?"

"I know what you mean."

"But then, the kids around here didn't know me last spring when it happened, so why should they have any feelings about it? As I said, to them it's history."

"Listen, the kids are already acting like that to me." I shivered and crossed my arms over my chest. "And I'm like you. I don't want them to talk, but when they don't, I think, *Oh yeah, just go on like nothing's happened.*"

Andrea frowned. "Is it us, I wonder, or is this normal?"

"I don't know." I shivered some more.

"Hey, you're freezing. Go back in the house. I'll call you tonight."

"Okay."

"So long." She started out, then turned and came back and gave me another hug. "We've got to stick together, right?"

"Right."

She pulled away. "Talk to you later."

She left and I went back inside and over to the fireplace. Sitting there, staring at the flames which flickered orange and blue, I wondered how many people were thinking what Andrea had said. Was Diane's death less of a tragedy because she'd brought it about herself? It didn't seem right. She was gone forever just the same.

But in doing it herself, Diane had left us with more than just her loss. She had tinged us all with a feeling of shame.

She was responsible. And so, it seemed were we. We shared in Diane's guilt. But how? I didn't know. I just didn't know.

══ 13 ══

I was dozing on the chintz sofa when Dad and Nell and Ned came back. Nell's high-pitched screeching, "I want to do mine now!" awakened me. Dad walked into the room and saw me and tried to shush the kids but I said it was okay, I wasn't really asleep. It would have been a lost cause if I had been.

"Nell," Dad said, "leave that out in the kitchen."

"But I want to show it to Bethany. Look! My Halloween jack-o'-lantern!"

Ned, coming along behind her, said, "It's not a jack-o'-lantern until you carve it, dummy. It's just a pumpkin now."

"Well, then, see my pumpkin," Nell said, pushing it practically into my face.

"Very nice," I said. "Take it back to the kitchen, Nell. And don't hold it by the stem. You could drop it." She and Ned both left.

"Where's Mother?" Dad asked.

I stretched. "Upstairs, sleeping, I hope."

He sat down beside me. "How was it?"

I shrugged.

"Pretty bad?"

I nodded. You should have gone along, I thought. But who would have taken care of the kids? Well, I could have. He should have gone.

Dad rubbed his hands back and forth on his knees, a thing he did when he was upset. "I know I should have gone, too," he said, softly enough so the kids in the kitchen couldn't hear. "But I couldn't seem to do it. I just can't. Not yet."

Ned's voice came from the kitchen, "Put that away, or I'm telling Dad!"

"What's going on out there?" Dad yelled.

Ned came to the doorway. "Nell's got a butcher knife. She says she's going to carve her pumpkin!"

"Nell, put it away!" Dad shouted. He made a move to get up.

"I'll go." Poor Father looked exhausted. He let the kids snow him, especially Nell. He'd give in to her until she got totally out of control and then he'd hand her over to Mom, saying, "I can't do a thing with her."

"Put that knife down!" I ordered as I walked in the kitchen and saw Nell at the table, the biggest knife of the set grasped in her fist.

She set her mouth with that stubborn look I knew so well. "Anyway, it's not the right kind of knife," I said.

Nell looked perplexed. I swooped and snatched it out of her hand.

"Give it back!" In a fury, she realized she'd been tricked. "I'll just get it again."

"I don't think you will, because you know very well

that if you cut yourself with a knife you'll miss out on all the Halloween fun." That was a really weak response but the best I could come up with on the spot.

Nell stuck out her lower lip and fell back on the standard, "I'm telling Mommy."

"Okay," I said cheerfully.

Nell slid down in the chair but made no move to go tattle.

Ned rolled his eyes to indicate how stupid Nell was.

"So where did you guys go today?" I asked him.

"We went to this place out in the country where people can go and pick apples if they want to. And they had this stand with cider and Indian corn and squash, or maybe they were gourds, and a great big stack of pumpkins. Hundreds of them. And we got to walk around and pick out whichever one we wanted."

"Sounds great."

"And we went to Dairy Queen," Nell said, not to be left out. "And I had a big chocolate frosty."

"I can see that," I said. "You're wearing part of it on your chin. Come on, let's wash it off."

Nell, agreeable now, got up and followed me to the small bath off the front hall. I had to say one thing for the kid. She didn't hold a grudge. Or could it be she just had an extremely short attention span?

That evening I was in my room making an attempt to study, without much success. My mind kept drifting to the bag of stuff in the closet, the smashed photo and bloodied paper towels. I knew I had to do something, make some attempt to find out what it was all about, or I'd never be able to focus on school assignments.

I'd look for Max's number. That was something to do.

I went through Diane's phone book. She always put numbers under kids' first names instead of last. No Max under *M*. Maybe this time she did it the other way. I didn't know Max's last name so I carefully went through each page. I found nothing.

Who'd know? The school office would, but I'd never have the nerve to ask the principal's secretary for the name and number.

Hope. She might. I dialed her number and when she answered I started out, "It's Bethany. Sorry to bother you again."

"No bother. What's up?"

"I decided to take your advice and talk to Steve and Max, but I can't find Max's number."

"I don't have it. And he's not at school this fall. He must have turned sixteen and cut out. Hmmm." After a moment she said, "I know what you can do. Call him at the pawnshop in Chicago. If he's not there, they can give you his number or something."

"I guess. But which pawnshop, Hope?"

"No idea. You'll just have to call around. Go down the list in the yellow pages."

My courage took a nose dive. Call a bunch of strange places? Well . . . I'd have to do it. "Hope? What exactly *is* a pawnshop? I mean, how do they get money?" I really didn't know.

"People take things there when they want to borrow

money," Hope said. "The pawnshop loans it to the guy and holds whatever he . . . or she . . . brings, as security. Then when the guy gets liquid again he goes back to the shop, repays the loan with interest, and reclaims his property. Got that?"

"I guess."

"Listen, Bethany, let me know how it turns out, will you?"

"Sure."

After we hung up I thought, *Sure, call that sleaze place of business, ask to talk to scurvy Max, ask him what he had to do with my sister's suicide. He's going to tell me just like that.*

I didn't know the guy, I didn't want to know the guy, but still I'd have to do this. But not right away. I was sure the place was closed anyway, on Sunday night.

I jumped when the phone rang, as though it could have been Max with some psychic insight, calling to say I was way off base.

It was Andrea. "How're you doing?"

"Good. Studying. Sort of."

"Would you rather keep at it?"

"You must be kidding. What's new?"

"I just talked to Chris again. He's so caught up in this party. It's going to be really wild."

"Good."

"I'm trying to think of a great costume. Something different, but not weird-ugly. Know what I mean? I'd rather look . . . now don't laugh . . . sexy."

"Wooo . . . ooo. Because of *him*. Go as a cigarette girl," I said.

"What's that?"

"Haven't you ever seen one in old movies? They carry around trays of cigarettes in nightclubs and wear skimpy clothes. You'd have to get some black fish-net stockings."

"My legs aren't all that great. Too muscular, from gymnastics."

"So wear something low-cut instead."

"My top isn't all that great, either. Have you thought of what you'll be?"

Absent, I wanted to say. I didn't see how I could go to the party and have any fun, but after Andrea and I had that tiff I didn't want to stir things up again. "I'm not sure," I said.

"Well, listen, I'll let you get back to the books, as I know you're just *dying* to do. Like I should. I hate homework. Teachers are sadists to make us study over the weekend."

"I know."

"So I'll see you tomorrow. S'long."

"S'long."

I hung up, opened my book, but the costume conversation had stirred up a memory and my eyes settled on Diane's bed. I could almost see her lounging on her back, one knee bent, arms flung over her head, the way I'd seen her just about a year ago. I was sitting here at the desk, like now, and trying to study then, too, but Diane was in a talkative mood.

"Did I tell you Steve and I are going to this fabulous Halloween party?" she said.

"A zillion times."

"But he doesn't like any of my costume ideas." She

stretched out then, and bent an elbow to support her head. "I think it would be spiffy to go as Antony and Cleopatra, don't you?"

"Depends on which one of you would be Cleo." I stared down at my opened lit book.

"Fool. It would be a real kick, the slithery costume and my hair in snaky coils, and tons of eye makeup, and a serpent coiled at my breast."

"Sounds adorable," I said. "Maybe Steve could be the snake."

"He doesn't mind the armor and helmet stuff but he had a fit when I told him a skirt is part of the costume."

"Skirt? Steve in a skirt?" I laughed.

"Oh, you're as bad as he is." She pulled herself up to the side of the bed. "I tried to get him to see that no one would notice the skirt . . . actually it's a covering for under the top part. And he'd wear lacings on his legs and whatever kind of shoes they wore—sandals maybe—but he just flat out refused. He can be so stubborn."

"So what will you go as, then?"

"I don't know. I'll think of something."

She did. I couldn't believe it later on when she said they were going as a bride and groom. "Steve doesn't mind?" I could see him taking all kinds of kidding.

"He doesn't have time to mind. The party's in just five days; it's practically showtime. Besides, this will be easy. Margo's borrowing a short bridal gown for me from someone she knows and Steve can get a waiter's outfit that looks like a tux from his uncle."

* * *

I'll never forget how Diane looked the night of the party.

Steve had gotten to our house before Diane was ready, and he sat in the living room with us, looking uncomfortable. I think the suit was a little tight through the shoulders. He had a bouquet of artificial flowers which he nervously jiggled up and down as though it were a basketball.

At a break in the conversation, he glanced at his watch again and then looked at the stairs and his mouth dropped open.

We all looked.

Diane was standing at the top of the stairs looking like someone from *Bride's* magazine. The dress was white and cocktail length and though it hadn't looked all that great on the hanger, with Diane inside it was a knockout. The headpiece on her dark, curled hair was like a wreath with sparkles on it, and it had a tulle bow in back and a little cascade of tulle ruffles. I can still picture her there at the top of the stairs, one hand on the banister, looking absolutely radiant, cheeks flushed and eyes full of wonder, as though she really were getting married.

Nell was the first to move. With a squealed, "Diane, you look beautiful!" she raced up the stairs, took her sister's free hand, and walked down with her, her face turned up toward Diane's.

Steve managed to meet them awkwardly, at the foot of the stairs, and after saying, "Here are your flowers," he thrust the bouquet at Diane. He looked blown away by her beauty, but at the same time a bit embarrassed at being a part of this all-too-real-seeming masquerade.

I think my parents were just as ill at ease, and I could understand why. There was their daughter, looking like a real-life bride at the age of fourteen.

After a moment or two, Dad cleared his throat and said, "Where's your coat, Diane? It's too chilly to go out like that."

Sounding like her regular self, Diane said, "Oh, Dad, don't be such a worrier. We'll just be getting in and out of the car."

Dad gave in. He drove Diane and Steve to the home of the kids throwing the party. I still remember his expression when he came back. He gave a half smile and said, "I was relieved to see there was actually a party going on."

"What?" Mom said.

"They looked so authentic . . . Diane and Steve . . . I half expected to see streamers on our car, and instead of a party, a wedding rehearsal in progress."

"Maybe in the back of their minds it *is* like a wedding rehearsal," Mom said. "But ten years in advance is stretching it, I'd say."

They both laughed, but beneath their lighthearted attitude it seemed to me they were strangely uneasy.

Remembering all this nearly a year later, I felt a chill. Did Diane sense that she would never live to be a bride, so this pretense was the next best thing?

I couldn't let myself believe that. It would mean that Diane had planned her death way ahead of time. I didn't believe that. I didn't.

The next day after school I went right to the kitchen
and hauled out the yellow pages to make a list of
names and numbers of pawnshops in Chicago.

Nell came home before I was finished and wanted
to know what I was doing. "Just a little project," I
said. "Why don't you go change your clothes?"

"Will you help me make my jack-o'-lantern?"

I marked my place on the page. "It's too soon, Nell.
If you carve it now, it'll be rotten by Halloween." Dad
shouldn't have let her get a pumpkin so early . . . like
three weeks too early . . . but he almost always caved
in when Nell went into her baby-doll "Oh, please,
Dad-dee!" routine.

Now she directed the full wattage of her baby
blues on me. "Please . . . please . . . Beth-ie . . . oh
please!"

I was as weak as Dad. Anyway, what did it matter?
"All right, Nell, but I'm telling you, you'll be sorry
when Halloween comes and your jack-o'-lantern is all

squishy and squashy." It might teach her a lesson. Unless Dad went out and got her another one.

"Oh . . . thank you!" she trilled, now all sparkly smiles.

The front door slammed and I looked out to see Ned, red-faced and angry-looking.

"Ned . . . what's wrong?"

"Leave me alone!" he shouted. He stomped upstairs and then I heard his door slam. Well!

I stepped back to the kitchen. Nell was bringing in her pumpkin from outside.

"What's the matter with Ned?" I asked her.

"I don't know." She plopped the pumpkin down on the table. "He's always fighting."

"Ned? Fighting? How come?"

"Don't ask me. I'm just the little sister." She was wearing a T-shirt with that message on it.

It wasn't like Ned to get into scrapes, but then all kids probably did at one time or another.

"Nell," I said, "please go change your clothes."

"Come with me?"

"No, I have to finish up here. Scoot, if you want me to help you."

I'd just put the telephone book away when she came back. Her old T-shirt was on backward. "I'm ready!" she said. "Let's make Mister Jack-o'-Lantern!"

I shoved the list I'd made into my jeans pocket and spread newspapers on the table. I plunged the knife into the top and cut out a jagged circle around the stem. When I let Nell pull off the lid, slimy strings and seeds came with it. I cut them off and then notched the lid for smoke to escape. "Okay, you can clean it out now," I said.

"How?"

"With your hands."

"But it's all mushy."

"Nell, that's the way it is. If you'd rather not, okay, we're finished."

Making a face, Nell pulled out the insides. After each handful she fastidiously picked off clinging seeds and orange goo. This would keep her busy for a long time.

I checked out Mom's dinner list for the week and saw we were slated to have lasagna tonight . . . all cooked and frozen, and pot roast tomorrow. I decided that as long as I was stuck in the kitchen anyway, I'd do the pot roast today and free up tomorrow. I had it ready to go into the oven and was peeling carrots and potatoes to go with it when Nell announced she was finished.

I checked out the pumpkin and saw, not surprisingly, that it was far from finished. I gave Nell a big spoon and told her to scrape. I knew she didn't have the strength to ream it out altogether but at least it would keep her busy until the roast was in the oven.

"Okay," I said some minutes later, sitting next to her. "Pick the best side now, for the face. Do you want a happy or a scary jack-o'-lantern?"

Nell looked like a flirty-eyed doll as she tried to make a choice. Then, "Happy," she said.

"All right, here's a pencil. Draw on a smile and we'll cut it out."

She drew the eyes and nose and stopped. "No, scary," she said.

"So make it scary." I went over and dug around in the refrigerator for a Pepsi. Then I switched to orange juice, just to set an example for Nell. The folks were trying to keep the kids from drinking too much soda.

Nell leaned back and looked at the pumpkin. "I've changed my mind. I'm going to wait for Halloween."

I rolled my eyes, sighed, and said, "Okay. I'll put it outside in some cool, shady spot." With luck, it would last.

I was going upstairs, Nell trailing after, when I heard the phone ring. I dashed into my room and grabbed it.

"Hi, it's Andrea. Got good news!"

"Oh yeh? What?"

"The party plans are really shaping up. A mob of kids are going to be there. It'll be such a blast!"

"Anyone from our school?"

"Oh, sure. Julie and Becky and Shelley are definitely coming and maybe Brandi and Cindi."

In a fake, guttural voice I asked, "Any . . . guys?"

"Are you kidding? Swarms. All of Chris's friends, practically."

I wanted to ask if that Harold . . . Mac . . . would be there but I didn't want to start anything.

"Listen, Beth, it's okay if you want to bring Kevin along."

"Kevin?"

"Your *friend? Kevin?"*

"I know who Kevin is, you ditz, but I just don't see

him at a party like that." I didn't want to say I couldn't see myself going to the party, either. I wasn't much in the mood and doubted that I would be three weeks from now. "Have you decided what you'll go as?"

"Probably a hippie. Elaine knows some shop where they have tie-dye stuff and I could easily rent one of those long wigs."

"Sounds good. And comfortable, too. I mean, better than being in, like, a gorilla costume where you get all stiff and sweaty."

After we hung up, I realized that Nell had been sitting at my desk, listening to it all. *"I'm* going to a Halloween party, too," she announced.

Ned's voice said, "You are not." He was hovering in the doorway.

"I am!" Nell said indignantly. "At my school!"

"Baby stuff," Ned said, edging into the room. He looked sullen.

"And I know what I'm going to be at my party!" Nell scrambled up on the desk chair and then leaped, small arms flying. "A cheerleader!"

I tried not to react, though the idea horrified me.

Ned came farther into the room. "You can't be a cheerleader. No one makes a costume to fit a peewee your size."

Nell screwed up her face at her brother. "Then Mommy can make me one!"

How could I get her to change her mind? She was too young to understand why her idea was so devastating, and she was a stubborn kid.

I decided to fall back on trickery. In an innocent,

offhand way, I said, "The other day I got an idea for the most beautiful costume in the whole world!" I sighed. "But it would have to be for a little girl, not for me. I'm too old."

Nell eyed me warily. "What?"

"I thought of a costume for Tinker Bell!"

Ned made a barfing sound. Nell didn't notice. Her eyes were fixed on me.

"It would be pink, with a wonderful skirt that stuck way out." I demonstrated. "And Tinker Bell would have a sparkly crown on her head, and she would carry a magic wand!" I demonstrated that, too, feeling every inch the phony.

Nell looked as if she were hooked.

I assumed a thoughtful expression. "Maybe I should tell your friend Laura about my idea, about Tinker Bell. She'd look so pretty." Then I smiled at Nell. "But of course, you'll look nice, too, in a scratchy red cheerleader sweater."

I could almost see the visions flitting about in Nell's mind as she stood there frowning, considering. Suddenly there was a breakthrough.

"You know what?" Nell said, quivering with animation. *"I* can be Tinker Bell!"

"You?" I said, astonished.

"Yes! I can be Tinker Bell!" Her voice was high, excited. "And I will have the magic wand!"

"Wow," I said. "That blows my mind. It really does!"

Nell began twirling around and around, chanting, "I will be Tinker Bell!"

I looked at Ned. He looked back at me and then

lowered his eyes. A little grudging smile appeared. He knew what I'd done; he probably even understood why. God, I love that kid.

Nell whirled into me and I grabbed her shoulders to stop her. "Cool down," I said, "or you'll be all tinkered out before Halloween even gets here."

She fluttered out of the room and Ned, too, went away. I felt vaguely troubled about him, about what was going on in his life. But he was such a private person. I'd better wait, let him reveal what he wanted to reveal in his own way, in his own time.

══ 15 ══

The next day at lunch hour, armed with lots of change, I went to a pay phone and called the first name on the pawnbroker list. Nervously, I asked if there was a *Max* working there.

"Max who?"

"I . . . uh . . . don't know."

"We don't have any Max working here."

Jerk. Then what did it matter, which Max? I dialed again and again. Always the same answer, no Max. As my stack of coins got smaller I began to wonder if this was such a hot idea. Then, suddenly, a bored voice answered with "Maximilian's."

"What? Isn't this"—I looked at my list—"Big M Pawn Brokers?"

"The same," he said. "What you got to pawn? Bring it in."

"This isn't . . . I don't . . . what I mean is, I'd like to speak to . . . Max?"

"Which one?"

"Uh . . ."

"The old one or the young one?" The voice sounded really bored.

"Uh . . . the young one, I guess." I was perspiring a little.

"Not here."

"Is he . . ." I wondered if he'd moved. "Is he there . . . sometimes?"

"Sometimes he is, sometimes he's not. Who's this calling?"

"Uh . . . a friend."

The voice altered. "He's got friends? This is news. What do you want with him?"

"Just to talk."

"He's not in trouble? Or got you in trouble?"

I felt a little unnerved. "No . . . nothing like that. I just want to talk with him."

"I'll see if I can locate Mister Big Shot."

There was a long silence. The operator asked for another fifteen cents. I dropped the coins in the slot. Finally I heard a little sound and then a voice said, "Max here. Who is this?"

"It's . . . it's . . . Diane's sister. Bethany?"

Pause. "Oh yes, the redhead." He must have seen me watching from a window when he came by the house. "What can I do for you?"

"Well . . . I'd like . . ." I pulled at my turtleneck that was making my neck damp. "I'd like to talk to you."

"Yeh? What about?"

"About Diane. See, I'm trying . . ."

He didn't help and I was getting more nervous. The

first bell was ringing in the hall and kids were coming by, making a lot of noise. "I was wondering if . . . if I could talk to you." Had I just said that?

"We're talking."

"I know, but I mean, like, in person?" And quickly, "I'm wondering if you come out here at all?"

"Never."

"Oh."

"So if you want to talk in person, it looks like you'll have to come here."

"To the city?"

"That's where I am."

Now it was so noisy in the hall I could hardly hear. "Okay," I said, before I could change my mind. "When?"

"You name it."

"Tomorrow?" Do it, get it over with.

"What time?"

"I . . . I'll have to look up the train schedule. Some time in the morning?"

"Okay. See you."

As I hung up I wondered how I'd do this. But there wasn't time at the moment to worry. I had to rush to get to my first afternoon class.

The next morning, riding along in a cab, I had the feeling that I was both watching a movie and taking part in it. Surely I couldn't be taxiing down a Chicago street on a school day, ditching classes, riding first a bus, next a train, and now this cab. It was wild, it wasn't me here, alone, going who knew where.

The driver, who had an accent, stopped the cab in front of the pawnshop, said, "This the place you wanted, sis?" and gave me a look when I told him it was and paid up. He probably thought I'd taken the family heirlooms and was about to pawn them so I could buy drugs. Oh, what did I care what he thought? I was nervous at the idea of going into the shop.

It had a kind of mesh antitheft covering over the windows. I could dimly see jewelry and electronics through the spaces. There was a button I had to press in order to get buzzed inside the shop.

An old guy behind the counter looked up from his newspaper, a skeptical expression on his face. I guess not many schoolgirls came into this place.

"I have an appointment with Max. The young Max," I said.

The man gave a one-sided grin and picked up an intercom. "Hey, Mister Hot Shot," he bellowed, "you've got someone with an *appointment* to see you." He lost interest, went back to his paper, and didn't even look up when Max strolled into the room.

Standing close to him, I realized how tall and thin he was. His dark hair, parted in the middle, hung to his shoulders. And if Max wanted to make a statement that he was different, his clothes shouted out the news. He had on black jeans, the long, loose white shirt I'd heard about, plus a man's pin-striped vest. He stood looking at me, indifferent, but at the same time a little wary.

"Hi," I said, a bit nervously. "I'm Bethany. The one who called?"

"I figured. Want to go someplace, have some coffee?"

"Sure. That's fine." My voice seemed steady but my knees were shaking.

Max glanced at the man behind the counter. "Going next door." The guy just grunted.

The coffee shop was an ordinary place with stools and booths. We sat in a booth and the waitress came right over with a pot of coffee, turning the thick waiting cups upright in their saucers. I pretended I drank coffee all the time.

"So what's all this about?" Max asked. His voice was low and just the least bit husky.

"Well . . . I'm trying . . . you know . . . to figure out why my sister Diane did . . . what she did, and I thought maybe . . ."

"I had some answers?"

"Right." And then quickly, "I don't mean to say you had anything to do with it, but I thought maybe . . ." I struggled for words. "You had some idea?"

Max looked at me for a moment before pouring artificial creamer into his coffee and stirring it. Was this the guy everyone said was so wild in his ways? He seemed more to me like someone who's been beat down a lot. "Bethany," he said, "I have no clue as to why your sister did it. I was as shocked as anyone when I saw it in the paper."

"The Chicago paper?" That surprised me.

"No, I stopped by my grandma's place one day to pick up some stuff, and there it was, in the *Suburban*

Times or whatever, on her kitchen table. Man, I couldn't believe it." He brushed his palm over one side of his hair. "I just couldn't believe it."

We sat in silence for a few moments. No one could believe it. "You didn't go to the . . . ?"

"Funeral home? No way. I don't believe in that stuff. I mean, I don't think it's decent, staring at someone when they're dead like that."

"I know." I drank some coffee, then said, "When was the last time you did see her?" I hoped I wasn't coming across like some juvenile police examiner.

"I'll never forget." Max frowned a little, paused, took a sip of coffee. "The last time I saw Diane was around the middle of August. She called and said she had to see me. She said I didn't understand. Well, she was the one who didn't understand. But I said, okay, I'd come out. I thought that way I could convince her once and for all."

"Convince her of what?"

"That we were finished."

"You were breaking up?"

"We were broken up. I knew it, but I guess Diane didn't. So I thought, okay, I'll have to prove it." Max looked down and moved his cup back and forth in the saucer. "But she thought she had another kind of proof." He shook his head. "That Diane. She was some kind of girl."

I felt jittery. "What kind of proof did she have?"

Max sighed. "I went over to your house, like she insisted. She was the only one there. And she started out right away saying she didn't care for Steve, and there was no point in my being jealous. Hell, I wasn't jealous. I wanted her to pick up with him again, get off my case. She didn't even give me a chance to say anything, though . . . she was all cranked up, acting crazy. And then she suddenly dashed upstairs and came back with this guy's picture . . ."

"Steve's picture?"

"Yeh . . . and she smashed the glass with her fist, and pulled out a broken piece of the glass and raked it along her arm. I just stood there for a minute, thinking, Oh, man, what kind of scene is this? I mean, weird city! And then I saw the blood oozing out."

My heart was thudding. "What did you do?"

"I ran out to your kitchen, grabbed some paper towels and wrapped them around her arm until it stopped bleeding. And all the time she was crying. Not from any kind of pain . . . I mean, she didn't even seem to notice the cut. She was going on about how I was the only one who mattered to her . . . stuff like that. And couldn't we get back together?"

"What did you tell her?"

"Well, I wasn't going to commit myself but I wanted to calm her down so I sat there next to her and talked. I told her we weren't necessarily finished for all time, but I thought we ought to call a short halt. Like, I was back in the city and she was about to start a new school year. And how she ought to make the most of it. Be Homecoming Queen, cheerleader, whatever did it for her, and really live it up."

"Did she go for the idea?"

"Yeh, I thought she did. She even got around to saying, finally, that she knew we were different and realized all along that it wouldn't last, but it had been fun hanging around with me. That kind of thing. By the time I left, she was really in a good mood." Max's lips twisted in a small smile. "I even remember one of the last things she said to me. She said, 'Some day, maybe I'll come into the shop and pawn my diamonds.' And I said, 'Naw, you'll never have to pawn any diamonds. You'll be too loaded. Like, rich and famous.'"

Rich and famous.

Max said, voice low, "When I left, I kind of wondered if I'd ever see her again. I remember thinking that." He reached into his pocket, dragged out a couple of bills and put them on the table. "Ready?"

I nodded.

Next door, he pressed the button, and when the door buzzed he opened it and held it slightly ajar. "Bethany? You seem like a very nice girl. I'm going to give you some advice for free."

I waited.

"Get on with your life. Don't let this business of your sister take over your mind."

"It hasn't."

He gave me a look. "Then why are you here?" He turned and went inside. The door locked itself behind him.

On the train ride home I went over and over in my

148

mind what Max had said, partly about Diane, and partly about his advice.

I *wasn't* letting Diane's death take me over. I was trying to find a reason, that's all. I couldn't put Diane's death to rest until I had gone over all the possibilities. I owed that to her.

Or did I owe it to myself?

16

By the time I got back to our suburb, school wasn't quite out yet so I arrived home a little early.

I walked into the house and my heart stopped. Mom was there! How had she found out? How well could I lie?

"Mom," I said, with a great show of innocence, "how come you're home so early?"

"The school called," she said. "I'm really upset."

Oh no. I wondered how much they knew. Surely they didn't have an inside tip about the pawnshop. I mean, this was only a school, not the C.I.A. "What did they tell you?"

"Nothing. They asked me to come by and talk to them in person, so I got someone to cover for me and went over."

How embarrassing! I could only hope no one I knew had seen her. My mother . . . going to see the principal! "Mom," I said, "I don't know what they told you, but there's an explanation. I didn't want to have to tell you and get you all upset, but . . ."

"You knew about it?"

"Knew about *what?*"

My mother looked at me as though I was some kind of mutant. "About Ned, of course."

"Ned?" I did a fast mental flip-flop. "Oh. Ned." What about Ned, I wondered. "What's he been doing that's so terrible?"

"I thought you said you knew. Oh, well." Mom slumped down on a kitchen chair. There were worry lines on her forehead. "He isn't concentrating in school, in fact his attention span is zero, and he's fighting with kids in his class."

"You mean arguing, or really mixing it up?"

"Physically fighting." Mom sighed deeply.

"Our Ned? That doesn't sound like him at all." My previous feeling of guilt had shifted into concern. "Do they have any idea why?"

"It's because of Diane." Mom folded her hands and then twisted them nervously. "The kids are saying things to Ned and he hits them when they do."

I sat down opposite her. "What kind of things?"

"Like . . . 'Your sister did something bad, really bad. So that makes you and your whole family bad, too.'"

"Oh, Mom."

"And Ned doesn't know how to answer, so he hits them. Today, several of them ganged up on him at recess and he got a bloody nose, and became hysterical."

Tears came to my eyes. My poor little brother. "Did you see him?"

"No, he was all right, I guess, by the time I got there.

The principal just wanted to see me alone, so I could do something about it." She made a little gurgling sound. "As though I know what to do."

I hesitated, then said, "Mom, I've always thought we should have talked to Ned and Nell instead of trying to cover up everything."

"They realize that Diane's dead."

"But not *how.*"

"Your father and I wanted to protect them. They're so young . . ."

"But Mom, they're not stupid. And people talk. The other kids know, and it's not fair to keep Ned in the dark, wondering why they're saying those things and what it all means."

"I guess. I guess we were wrong not to discuss it with them." Mom got up and replugged the coffeepot. "My poor babies. They're both suffering. This thing has hit us all, hasn't it? And what do we do now?"

"You said *babies.* Are kids picking on Nell, too?" I felt like going out and bashing a few small heads myself.

"No, with Nell it's something else. Nightmares. Haven't you heard her at night? I try to get to her before she wakes everyone else up. Sometimes I have to sleep with her. Sometimes she wets the bed. That reminds me . . ." She started to get up.

"What?"

"I have to go down and put her sheets in the dryer. I stuck them in the washer this morning. That makes three times this week."

"Mom, I'll go. Take it easy." I went downstairs. The

152

dread of going to the basement wasn't as bad now, since we'd gotten rid of the brown couch, but still it wasn't my favorite place.

I dragged out the Bo-Peep printed sheets and stuck them into the dryer. I'd had no idea Nell was so upset. To me, she'd seemed the same lighthearted girl she'd always been. It was scary, the way our family's hidden feelings were showing up, now, suddenly.

When I came back upstairs and saw what Mom was doing, I stopped, shocked.

"What?" she said, seeing the look on my face.

"You're smoking!"

Mom gave a tiny laugh.

"You haven't smoked for . . . for about ten years!"

"I'm nervous. This seems to help."

"It's not going to help. And you'll get lung cancer. Mom, you're a *nurse,* for Pete's sake!"

"All right." Mom ground out the cigarette, then reached into her purse and took out the almost empty pack and handed it to me. I was going to pulverize these last four in the disposal, but trusted Mom enough to just toss the pack into the garbage.

Right now I had a little moral advantage so I decided it might be a good time to tell Mom about my day. "Before you find out, I'd better brief you myself, about what I did today. I cut all my classes."

"You did? Why?"

I saw I had ten or fifteen minutes before the kids were due home so I got a can of Pepsi, pulled off the tab, and leaned against the counter. "I went into Chicago to see Max."

"Max?"

"Yes, you know, that kid Diane was chasing around with all summer."

"I knew *of* him, but I could never pin your sister down as to who he was, what he was." She gave me a look. "Was he mixed up with Diane's . . . death? What's all this about?" Her voice was getting urgent. "What did this Max have to do . . . tell me, Bethany!"

"Mom, relax. He had nothing to do with it."

"Then why did you have to go into Chicago to . . . I just don't understand this at all!"

"Mom, if you'll just take it easy, I'll tell you. I had to go into Chicago because that's where Max is living again. I felt I had to talk to him, find out if he knew anything at all that would help us . . . you know . . . to understand. . . ."

"And what did he say?"

"Not much." I took a swig of soda. "He said Diane was upset when he told her they ought to break up." The image of Diane cutting her arm came to me but I saw no reason to lay that story on Mom, at least not right now. Maybe later, when things . . . I went on, "He said that the last time he saw Diane she was in a pretty good mood."

"What kind of person is this Max?" Mom twisted her fingers through the handle of the coffee mug.

"He's actually not bad. Everyone at school thought he was a scuzz, but I think he acted eccentric because he knew the kids weren't going to approve of him anyway."

"Except for Diane."

"Yeh, well, I think he appealed to her because he was different. Dangerous. You know Diane . . . always out for a kick of some kind." I paused. "Or *was.*"

"Lately I've been thinking I didn't really know Diane," Mom said. "And wondering if I'd only . . ."

"Mom, don't start blaming yourself. You were great to Diane and she was crazy about you. She loved you more than . . ."

"Don't say it. I don't want to hear that."

Well, she did anyway, I thought. I glanced at the clock. "So what are you going to say to Ned?"

"I don't know."

"Mom, maybe you should take him to a psychiatrist or someone."

"I've thought of that." She got up, put the mug in the sink, and picked up her purse. "I may give a doctor I know at the hospital a call. I just know we can't go on like this. We need help. All of us. We need to build up some defenses."

Just as she left the front door slammed and I heard Mom say, "Hi there, honey. Now, don't rush off like that. I want to talk to you."

And Ned said in a low, guarded tone, "What about?"

"Different things. Where's Nell? Oh, here she is. Why don't we all go upstairs?"

After they were out of earshot I dialed Hope's number, muttering "Be there, be there." And then, as she answered, "Hey, guess what. I did it! I went into Chicago on my own and found Max and talked to him!"

"Yey! What a woman!" she said with some jubilance. "What did he tell you?"

"Lots. Remember the bloody paper towels and the smashed glass and the photo?"

"Sure."

"Max said he came to the house some time in August . . . no one was home except Diane . . . and he suggested they break up. Diane thought Max was just jealous of Steve, so to prove she didn't like him anymore, she . . ."

"Smashed his photo and raked her arm with a piece of the glass."

"Right."

"It sounds like something Diane would do. Real dramatic. What did you think of Max?"

"You know, I liked him. He was really nice to me. I felt a little sorry for him, actually. The guy in the shop treated him like dog meat."

"Does he live right there in the pawnshop?" Hope asked. "How was it, by the way?"

"It looked like a regular store, only messier, and with grates over the windows. I don't know where Max lives. He didn't say."

"What else did he tell you?"

I thought. "Nothing much, I guess, except that when he left, Diane seemed in a good mood. She said that some day she'd come in and pawn her diamonds."

"What diamonds?"

"The ones she'd have when she was rich and famous."

"Oh . . ." Hope said in a small voice. "That's so sad."

"I know." The vision of Diane's grave with the faded flowers came into my mind.

After a brief silence Hope said, "Diane always expected things to come to her. She wasn't conceited . . . at least I never thought she was. But she did have a certain attitude. It was almost as though she put herself a little bit apart. As though some rules didn't actually apply to her."

And in a rush I thought, *Including the laws of nature. In her heart Diane didn't really think she could die.*

Hope was talking on. ". . . got by with things because of her charm. When we were little she even had me dazzled but I grew out of it, learned to walk away."

"Like Max did," I said. "And Steve."

"Not like them," Hope said. "I always came back."

"I wonder if Steve would have, eventually. I hate to think of talking to him."

"Then why do it?"

"I just have to. I have to . . . I don't know . . . touch all the bases. I can't stop halfway."

"And then what? After you've talked to Steve. What if he can't give you the answer you're looking for, either?"

"I don't know. What do you think I should do, Hope?"

She hesitated. Then softly, she said, "I think you should get on with your life."

It was the second time I'd been told that in just one short day.

17

Mom called the school office to excuse my absence. Afterward, she said to me, "It's okay this time, but don't take off like that again."

"I won't. What did Dad say about Ned?"

"He agrees that we have to do something. For Nell, too. I'm going to make some calls today."

At school, my friends, assuming I'd been out for sickness, asked how I was and when I said, "Good," that was the end of it. This was at lunch. The big topic was the Halloween party, now just two weeks away.

Andrea was definitely going as a hippie. Rebecca said she might go as a flapper. Julie observed that she had the chest for it—flat—and Rebecca dumped a bunch of catsup on Julie's fries. Sometimes they acted like fifth graders.

"How about you?" Andrea asked me. "Have you decided yet?"

"Not really." I hated to say I might not even go.

"You'll think of something," Julie said, smiling. "You're so creative."

"Oh, right." I asked who else was going.

"I don't know about Cindi and Shelley," Andrea said. "But Brandi definitely is. She's taking Darryl."

"I'm not asking any of the skuzzballs from around here," Julie said. "I intend to check out Chris's friends. They'd better be cute, Andrea, or else!"

I thought, *That's another reason I may not go. Everyone will be pairing up, or at least giving it their best shot. I don't want to play that game. I'm not ready.*

The afternoon dragged. I was still finding it hard to concentrate in my various classes. I couldn't seem to shake free of outside thoughts.

I decided I'd better talk to Steve and get it over with. It kept going through my mind that he might have the answer. Or if he didn't, he could still say something. Something that might mean nothing to him, but that could give me a new insight.

So stop stalling, I told myself. Go do it. You'll never feel satisfied until you've at least made the effort.

Later that day in chemistry class, I said to Kevin, "I know I've been a real nothing as your lab partner."

"You've been all right." He lowered the flame of the Bunsen burner. "Your lab reports are up to date."

"Thanks to you."

He took off his glasses and used his thumbnail to scrape a fleck of something off the lens. "I think you're doing great. Not many girls . . . or guys either . . . could go through what you've gone through and stayed so strong." He put his glasses back on.

"Thanks." I stooped to check supplies in the cabinet. As my eyes roved over the test tubes and other things I heard myself saying, "Would you want to go to a Halloween party?" *What was I saying!* I don't know who was more surprised, Kevin or me.

After a pause, he said, "Party? Where?"

I stood back up. "Over in the suburb where Andrea used to live. Her boyfriend Chris is throwing it." I wished I hadn't said *boyfriend*.

"And I'm invited?" Kevin looked puzzled.

"I'm inviting you. They said to bring anyone I wanted to."

Kevin was trying to look cool, but he couldn't keep the glow from his face. "Is it a costume party?"

"Right. But I don't suppose they'd call the sheriff if you turned up without one."

"Well . . . gee." Kevin still seemed to be trying to hold back, and it hurt me to think what a big deal this must be for him. "Are you sure? I mean, isn't there someone you'd rather take?"

"Don't be stupid," I said. "Oh, it looks like we need another twenty-five-milliliter beaker. We'd better put in a request before next class."

Because of different classes and schedules, I seldom saw Steve around school. I hated to call him at home, in case someone else answered and I'd have to leave a message. So I decided to stake out the main entrance to the school as kids were arriving. I got there early one morning and waited and waited.

There were five minutes to go before I had to leave for my first class when Steve finally showed up. To my great relief, he was alone. I hurried over and blocked his way so he had to stop.

"Hi, Steve. I need to talk to you."

"Oh? What about?" He gave a quick look over his shoulder.

"Things," I said.

"Yeh? What kind of things?" He glanced around nervously again. When I didn't answer, he shifted his books and said, "You mean, like Diane?"

"Yes. Like Diane." He was acting like a jerk.

"Hey, Bethany, I'm really sorry about what happened, but I don't know anything about it. I wasn't there, you know."

It had never occurred to me that he might have been. "Steve, I just want to talk to you, to get some input. It's bad enough that it happened, but it's worse not having any idea why. I'd hoped that you would at least. . . ." My voice broke a little.

Steve edged back a step. "Sure, Beth, I get it. And I'd really like to help you out . . ."

Before he could go on I said, "Good. Do you want to stop by the house?"

"No! I mean, I don't think it's a good idea. Look. Some day after school when there's no practice. . . ."

"When would that be?" I wasn't about to let him get away.

"Tomorrow. I'll meet you here. After last class. We can go somewhere. Talk." He backed up. "Okay?"

"Tomorrow. Fine." It was strange. Steve had always been so confident, so sure of himself, but now I was in control, watching him squirm.

The next day, as I waited for him, I began to wonder if Steve was ducking out on me. Bunches of kids went by, but no Steve. Finally, when the corridor was empty, he suddenly appeared with an air of *let's get this over with.*

"Where should we go, to talk?" I asked.

"How about back on the bleachers?"

"Okay." It was chilly outside, but still sunny, and I guessed in back of the school was as good a place as any to talk without being stared at or overheard.

"So how have you been?" he said as we went along toward the vacant playing field.

"Rotten."

"Oh, yes. Because of . . ."

"Yes, because of."

The gate wasn't locked and there was no one around as we made our way to the first bunch of bleachers. I leaned against the end of about the third row, hugging my books to my chest. Steve plopped down his books on the next row up, braced his hand against a riser and said, "So what did you want to tell me?"

"Tell you? I want you to tell *me.* Did Diane talk to you, give you any kind of hint? Just before . . . you know . . ."

"Me?" Steve's eyebrows shot up. "Are you kidding? We weren't even going together. You ought to know that. So why would we talk?"

"People can break up and still *talk.*"

"Well, we didn't. At least not that day. I didn't even see Diane, as a matter of fact. I can't remember the last time I saw her."

The words were hardly out of his mouth when he flushed. I knew he and I were both picturing the same scene . . . Diane at the funeral home. Lying there in her yellow dress, so quiet, so unreal, so . . . dead. I

162

could still see Steve, white-faced, staring at her, and Heather, after a quick glance at Diane, looking anxiously at Steve. Diane would have hated having Heather there, with Steve. But then, Diane had no say in things anymore. She had given up all rights when she decided to die.

"Did you know she and Max had split up?"

"Yeh, she let me know."

"Did Diane want to get back with you?"

"She didn't say it in so many words, but I got the idea."

"And you wouldn't?"

"Hey, I've got my pride. Besides, if you want the honest truth, I'll tell you. Your sister was like a little kid, real immature."

"I don't know what you mean," I said coldly, out of loyalty.

"I'll spell it out for you. A year ago, Diane got me to break up with Heather, right? And then Diane told me we needed to be together a lot, to build up a strong relationship."

I nodded. It sounded like Diane. She liked exclusive rights, especially when it came to people.

"So we were together a lot, the way she wanted. You saw that yourself."

Again, I had to nod. Diane and Steve logged more time together than astronauts in a space capsule. Everyone thought of them as a pair.

"And things were going along great until that sleaze showed up. Max. I used to have a dog by that name. Then suddenly I began getting a whole new routine from Diane. She said we had to be sure that we were

163

right for each other. We had to test our love. Those were her exact words." In a girlish voice Steve said, "We have to test our love."

I had to admit that it sounded like Diane, all right. She could always make up a good reason for what she wanted to do.

"So the next thing I knew, Diane was running wild with that slimebag, and no one could figure out his appeal, what was so wonderful about him. Why she'd . . ."

"Give you up for him?" I tried not to sound sarcastic, but I guess a little of it came through.

"All I'm trying to say is, it was her choice. And then, after she realized what a jerk he was, and dumped him, she wanted to get back with me."

I knew that actually it was Max who'd done the dumping, but I wanted Steve to go on with his story. "Did you tell Diane you didn't want to go back with her?"

"Not exactly. What I told her was that I was too busy testing my love with Heather."

I must have looked shocked. Steve said defensively, "Maybe I shouldn't have said it, but you know, I have my pride."

"You mentioned that before."

"Yes, well that was it."

"That was it."

Steve picked up his books. "So that's all I can tell you."

"One thing."

Steve turned. "Yeh?"

"How long before Diane died did you have this conversation?"

"Long before. Two or three weeks."

"How did she take it?" I tucked my books under an arm and together we walked out of the playing field.

"You know Diane. First she put Heather down, called her an airhead, that kind of thing, and then she went on about how she and I were right for each other, always had been, always would be. But then she calmed down and we left each other as pretty good friends."

It sounded right. I knew myself that Diane could get riled up and rant and rave, but then after she'd gotten it out of her system she'd be pleasant, almost casual.

Now that he was out of the witness box, so to speak, Steve seemed to relax. "What's this all about? I mean, what are you getting at?"

"It's not just you, Steve. I've been talking to several people, hoping to get a clue as to why Diane did it."

"In my opinion, it was an accident. I don't think she really meant to do it."

"If I could only be sure. . . ."

"Bethany, let it go. It happened. Get on with your life."

I bit my lip. Why was everyone saying the same thing?

By now we'd reached the sidewalk in front of the school. "Steve, thanks for meeting me," I said. "Thanks for talking."

"Hey, I only wish I could have helped." Steve gave me a small smile. "Well, so long, Beth. Take care."

I nodded and walked off in the opposite direction. *Take care of what?* I felt so down. How was I supposed to get on with my life? Suddenly, I heard footsteps from behind. I turned. It was Steve.

"I wasn't going to tell you this . . ."

"What?" We stopped, faced each other.

He looked around as though someone could be hidden in the bushes, with a secret mike. "The truth is, I'd about decided to get back with Diane."

I stared at him. "But you didn't tell her?"

"No, I didn't tell her. I was waiting for the right time. And she didn't seem to be hurting for attention. Guys were always hanging around her. I guess I wanted to be sure she wasn't going with someone else. Was she?"

"I don't think so." I swallowed. If only Steve had . . .

"I know what you're thinking," he said. "And I guess you want me to feel responsible, but I don't."

"It's not that . . ."

"I'm sorry your sister died," Steve said. "Really sorry. She was a neat kid. I liked her a lot. I guess you could say I . . ." his voice broke. "Loved her. But why did she have to be the way she was? Wanting it all to go her way? Expecting it all to go her way?"

"I don't know, Steve."

"A girl you've been so close to, doing what she did. . . ." A muscle quivered in Steve's cheek. He seemed about to cry. "It's hard to realize that Diane actually killed herself." He looked away. "But I can't let it ruin my life. I can't."

"You're right. It shouldn't."

"Why did she have to do it?" Tears came to his eyes. He blinked. "Look what she's done to everyone."

"I know." I clenched my lower lip in my teeth, trying to hold on.

"Everyone. Everyone who knew her. God, I feel so sorry for your family." Now tears were spilling down Steve's cheeks and suddenly, clumsily, with our books in our arms, we held each other in a hug. We pulled away then, and wiped the tears. "You can't let it ruin your life, either," he said. "Give it up, Bethany. There are no answers."

"I know. At least, I guess I know."

We made sorry attempts at smiles, and with mutual "See yous," we went our separate ways. We'd see each other again, sure, but we would probably never talk again. Steve would get on with *his* life. And yet I knew that no matter what, there'd always be a little spot in his mind where Diane would stay. She'd marked him as she'd marked all of us, that day she suddenly decided that dying was the thing she'd do.

167

The next day Mom asked me if I was planning anything for Friday night. When I said I wasn't, she asked if I'd be willing to go to the psychiatrist with her and Dad.

"Why me?" I asked. "I thought it was Nell and Ned you were worried about."

"I am, but she . . . the therapist . . . wants us to see this psychiatrist before she sees the kids."

I agreed. Friday night they got a sitter for the kids and the three of us went to the psychiatrist's home.

She lived about a half hour away, in another suburb. Her house was nice . . . modern, lots of glass . . . and the room she led us into was cheerful with its patterned sofa and chairs and soft lighting. I could have curled up and read there quite happily.

"Tell me about Diane," Doctor Harris said. She had dark hair and eyes, nice figure, pleasant voice. "Bethany, how did you see your sister?"

"Pretty," I said. "Lively. She had lots of friends, was very popular."

"With both girls and boys?"

"Yes. She always had lots of kids around her. Or else she was on the phone with them."

"How did you feel about that?"

"About what?"

"Her popularity."

I wondered what I was supposed to say. I shrugged. "It was fine."

"Would you say you're like Diane?"

"Me? Not at all."

"How are you different?"

I looked over at Mom and Dad on the sofa, as though they were the ones who should answer. They didn't. "I'm more quiet. I like to read. I enjoy art. Things like that."

"And how do you feel, now that Diane's no longer there?"

"I feel lonely at times. Cheated." *Why did I say that?*

"Cheated?" She looked at me sympathetically.

"Yes." Tears came to my eyes. "I feel cheated that she isn't there for me."

"And perhaps a little angry at times?"

"Yes." Now I was starting to cry. It surely hadn't taken long.

"Bethany, it's all right to feel cheated, angry. Someone you love has been taken away. You feel deprived."

"I just keep asking myself. . . ." I looked around blindly and saw there was a box of tissues on the table. I took a couple. "I keep asking myself *why?* Why did it have to happen?"

"In suicides, the question of *why* is always there,"

the doctor said. "Especially when there's no note. You can't understand why someone would choose to leave you, with no explanation."

"I . . . I keep thinking I should have known she was unhappy. I should have seen that, and done something to help her."

"You are not responsible. You must believe that. Not you or anyone else. It was Diane's decision."

"If I hadn't worked," Mom said in a weepy voice, "if I had been home . . . I can't help it, I keep thinking I should have been there."

After a pause, the woman said, "If you had been home, would you have followed your daughter to the basement, if you thought she was going down to do the laundry?"

"No."

"Would you have followed her everywhere she went?"

"Well . . . no."

"So you see, you couldn't have been her watchdog. She could have done it any time. At night, for instance, after everyone else was asleep."

Dad spoke up. "I thought by now the pain would subside just a little. But it's there every day. It hurts. My God, it hurts."

Now all three of us were crying. Doctor Harris sat patiently, letting us get it out of our systems. "Of course it hurts," she said gently.

· "It's so hard to come home," Dad said, "and know she's not there. And to have to pretend, for the sake of the children."

"Why must you pretend?" she asked.

"Well . . ." Dad looked bewildered. "Because I don't want to upset them. They're too young to have to go through that."

"How much do you think they understand?" The doctor frowned slightly. "What have you told them?"

Dad looked at Mom. She said, "Just that Diane is dead."

"And do they know about death?"

After a silence I said, "I don't think they do. Not really. And especially not about the way she died." I remembered Nell lying on the couch downstairs, play-acting Diane's death. "I don't think they've even asked, at least not me. Have they asked you, Mom? Or you, Dad?"

They both said no.

The doctor nodded. "It sounds as though they sense that there's a taboo on that subject. If they asked it might make you angry, or upset. So they play along in the game of silence. That's what children do, you know."

We went along talking like that for a while. It felt so good to be open at last, to confess to feelings we'd all tried to hide, but which, it turned out, were quite normal.

I looked at Mom and Dad sitting there, looking drained, but still more at peace than I'd seen them for a long time. I felt that we'd all turned a corner, that we were taking the first real steps to recovery.

And then it happened.

I'd finished describing that awful Friday afternoon when I found her downstairs on the couch.

171

"Was this Diane's first attempt?" Doctor Harris asked.

Without really thinking, I said, "No." At the same time Mom said, "Yes."

The doctor looked at each of us. "Which is it?"

I felt frozen. "She . . . kind of tried once before," I stammered, "but . . ."

"What?" Dad said, lurching forward. "When was that?"

His expression scared me. Mom was hunched back on the sofa, her face white and frightened-looking.

Oh God. What had I done?

"I asked *when*. Answer me, Bethany!"

I looked at Doctor Harris but she was like someone at a play . . . interested but not taking part.

"It was more than six months ago. Diane took just a few pills . . . not many, you know."

"Go on."

"Well, she . . ." What was I supposed to say! "She got over it."

Without expression, Mom said, "Diane called me at work. I came home, made her vomit, gave her coffee, kept her awake."

"And you didn't see fit to inform me about it!" Dad yelled. "My own daughter!" He leaped up, went to the door and flung it open. "You two!" His look of contempt nearly shattered me.

"Mr. Kingsley?" The psychiatrist got up and followed Dad. We could hear her say, "You'll never deal with this by walking away. I know you've had a shock. But please come back. Talk it out."

"Yeh, what should I say? You two hid a suicide

attempt I had every right to know about, but that's okay?"

"Not unless that's how you really feel."

After a moment he returned and sat at the far end of the sofa, away from Mother. "I feel like hell, that's how I feel. Why didn't they tell me?"

Dr. Harris looked at me. "Dad—(I wondered if he'd hate me so much he'd tell me not to call him *Dad* anymore)—we didn't want to upset you."

In a sarcastic tone he said, "Well, wasn't that considerate. . . ."

"You were having office problems. . . ."

"And the two of you decided that was top priority in my life? More important than my daughter trying to kill herself?"

I couldn't hold back any longer. I folded my arms tightly against my chest but the sobs wouldn't stay inside. I started shaking with them.

"Don't blame Beth," Mom said, staring ahead, and then, in that same emotionless voice, "I told her to keep quiet about it."

"That was your decision as a nurse?" Dad said. "Very professional."

"It was my decision as a wife."

"Well, thanks, but I don't need that kind of wife."

I felt a jab. What did Dad mean?

"I'm very sorry," Mom said, stiffly. "I know now it was wrong. But at the time . . ."

"If you're asking for forgiveness, forget it," Dad said furiously.

"I'm not asking for forgiveness. I'm asking for understanding."

173

"Huh!"

After a brief silence, the doctor said, "Mr. Kingsley, would you say you had a close relationship with your daughter Diane?"

"You bet!"

"And did she come to you with her problems?"

"Yes. Sometimes."

"When?"

"How can I tell you when? Sometimes."

"If, for instance, Diane was upset about some school situation or perhaps a boy-girl problem, did she come to you or her mother?"

"For those things she went to her mother."

"You mean . . . her birth mother?"

"Are you kidding? Margo?"

Dr. Harris gave a slight smile and leaned forward. "If your wife had come to you and told you that your daughter had taken some pills, what would you have done?"

"I'd have straightened her out. Diane."

"How?"

For the first time Dad looked unsure. "For one thing I'd have talked to her. Asked what was wrong."

"What if she couldn't tell you what was wrong?"

"Well . . . at least I would have tried."

"And do you believe that would really have made a difference?"

"It would to me," Dad said. "I'd have tried." He leaned forward and put his face in his hands. With a muffled sob he repeated, "I'd have tried."

Everyone was quiet for a few moments. Then Dr. Harris said, "I think this is enough for tonight. You're all exhausted. You've opened up subjects you didn't mean to, and now you have to deal with them." She stood up. "I think we should all meet again, in a week. There are more things to resolve, more feelings that need to be expressed."

"What about the little children?" Mom asked.

"Why don't you go ahead and make an appointment with the therapist? She uses play therapy, you know. She's very good."

At the front door, as we were leaving, Dr. Harris said, "Try to bear up. It does get easier. It does get better."

But first it got worse.

Mom had recovered enough by the time we were driving home to yell at Dad when he yelled at her. I shrank in the back seat, hands over my ears.

They quieted down before we got into the house, thank goodness. Dad took the sitter home. By some miracle, both Nell and Ned were asleep.

I went straight to my room. I heard Dad come back and then him and Mom saying things . . . not exactly arguing, but not making nice conversation, either. Then I heard them come upstairs . . . no, just Mom, because I heard her say, "It's all right, I understand. . . ." and then go into their room and close the door.

Would Dad want to get a divorce over this? If he did, would he ask for custody of Nell and Ned? He could say that Mom was an unfit mother. Not that she was, but he could say it.

I lay there thinking how messed up our whole

family was, and wondering if we'd ever get it together again. I'd thought when Diane died that the worst thing that could happen had happened. Now I wasn't so sure.

It was three A.M. when I awakened. Was it a sound, or what? I didn't hear anything. Cautiously, I got out of bed and opened my door. Silence.

Was Dad gone? Had he driven off in the night?

I listened again. Nothing. I crept quietly down the stairs; my eyes were getting used to the dark. The patio lights reflected softly into the living room. I could see Dad stretched out on the sofa. He rose up. "Beth?"

"Yes," I said in a low voice.

"What's the matter?"

"I . . . I . . . just wanted to see if . . ."

"Come here," he said just above a whisper.

I went over and sat down beside him. "I was afraid . . . you had left."

"Well, why would I do that?"

"Do . . . do you hate me?"

"Hate you? Beth. How could I hate you?"

"Do you hate Mother?"

"No, honey. I'm upset with her. I don't hate her."

"She didn't mean to hurt you."

"I know. But I do feel wounded. I know I shouldn't, but I do."

"Will you go back upstairs?"

"Not right now, Bethy. I have to be alone. I have to be alone and let the thoughts about Diane kind of settle in my mind." He kissed me on the forehead.

"You go back and get some sleep. Don't worry. We all love each other and that's what counts. We'll work things out."

At least the folks did agree that Nell and Ned should begin the therapy sessions right away. They were to go twice a week.

I was curious about what went on, but we'd been told not to ask the kids outright. If they wanted to talk about it, fine, but otherwise we should just leave it alone until they were ready to share.

Naturally, Ned didn't reveal a thing, but Nell, sitting at Diane's desk one day, drawing, said, "I smacked the Diane doll and said, 'You're not supposed to be dead! I am very angry with you. Yes, very angry!'"

"Are you going to stay angry?" I asked.

Nell put a crayon against her mouth while she looked off in space, thinking. "No, I guess not," she said, and went back to her drawing.

I wondered if my parents would stay angry at each other. During the days that followed the big fight they talked and tried to act natural, but still the warmth was gone. I hoped this wouldn't last forever. I couldn't imagine our living together if the love was no longer there.

One evening, Mom was reading to the kids and Dad was downstairs in his computer room. I felt so . . . I don't know . . . stretched apart.

I hated to think of him in the basement alone, even though I knew he had some work to do. I went down, and when he looked up, inquiringly, I said, "Hi, Dad. What're you doing?"

"Just some forms that came in a bunch today. What's on your mind?" He nodded at a chair.

I sat down. What could I say? I said the first thing that occurred. "Nell and Ned had another therapy session today."

"Yes, I know. It seems to be helping them, don't you think?"

"Yeh, really. I am curious to know what exactly goes on. What does?"

Dad frowned slightly. "Why don't you ask your mother?"

"I thought you'd know, too." Wow. The things that just pop out when you're not thinking.

Dad switched off the computer and leaned back in his chair. He was quiet. Then he said quietly, "Yes, I should know. But I just assumed your mother would handle it." A short silence. "I didn't even ask." At these last words he turned and looked at me. And the unspoken words between us were, *There you have it*.

After a few uncomfortable moments I stood up. "Well, guess I'll do some homework. Good night, Dad, if I don't see you later."

"Wait a minute." Dad reached over to switch off his desk lamp. "I'm going up, too. To hell with all this stuff. I'll get up early and do it."

Mom looked up, mildly surprised to see us, but she kept on reading to Nell and Ned. Dad sat beside them on the sofa. At first, Nell and Ned gave him uneasy glances, but then, seeing it was all right, all four of them seemed to relax and blend into a unit of warmth. I stayed, too, and listened to the rest of the story. When it was over, I got up, kissed them all good night, and went upstairs.

For the first time in a long while, I believed our family was going to be all right.

19

It seemed to me that all my friends were going boy-crazy. Brandi had invited Darryl to the Halloween party, but Julie and Rebecca said they weren't going to tie themselves down with dates. They were going to check out the guys at the party, just in case. Of course, Andrea would be with Chris. It got tiresome, hearing them go on about guys during every lunch hour, and then on the phone at night.

They knew I'd invited my friend and lab partner. They assumed I'd done it for humane purposes. Julie, in fact, said, "It's so sweet and self-sacrificing of you to invite poor Kevin."

"Why do you say 'poor Kevin'?"

Julie shrugged. "You know what I mean."

"Lighten up, you guys," Brandi said. "It's only a party, not a dating game." Easy for her to say, with Darryl wrapped around her finger.

The talk shifted to the next most popular topic: costumes.

So far, Andrea was going as a hippie and Rebecca

had definitely decided to be a flapper from the Roaring Twenties. At first Julie said she was going to wrap herself in foil and go as a baked potato, but the idea didn't seem very glamorous. Now she told us her Mom was going to rent a cancan dancer's costume for her.

Brandi said her father suggested she go as a bottle of brandy, but she was looking for something with a little more sex appeal.

I hadn't come up with an idea, and the party was only a week away. Sometimes I still wondered if I should go. But then I realized I had to go because in that weak moment I'd invited Kevin. I couldn't remember ever seeing him so excited over something that didn't involve beakers, test tubes, or chemicals.

I'd been talking to Kevin a lot on the phone lately. He was the one I always seemed to call when I was in a melancholy mood. If I was using him, he didn't appear to mind. Never once, when I talked to him about Diane, did he so much as hint that I should talk about something else.

My friends didn't exactly say it, but I could tell they were ready to drop the subject of my dead sister. I could understand that. I mean, they had helped me through my grief, but that time was over. They wanted to go on to lighter things, now. Fun things.

Even Andrea, who'd been so close and sharing after the suicide, now seemed to pull away from the subject. She'd put in more time than I had, though. Her brother's death was last spring. She was beginning to bloom again. Why should she let me drag her down?

It wasn't that I wanted to wallow in suffering and

sorrow. I just couldn't fling off the sadness. All I could do was put it aside now and then.

It was hardest for me to bounce back the day after the grief therapy meetings I was going to with Mom and Dad. I mean, you spend a couple of hours along with other people who have lost a child, wringing out your heart, and it leaves you a little weak. But each time it was a little easier to shake off the aftereffects.

At our final session with the psychiatrist in a spirit of openness, I'd gone over my talks with Hope and Max and Steve. "None told me exactly what I wanted to hear, though."

Dr. Harris asked, "Bethany, have you ever used a cash machine?"

What was this? "No, but I've been with Mom when she has."

"Do you remember the procedure?"

"You punch in numbers and answer questions, and the cash comes out."

"You see how simple it is with machines," the doctor said. "You press buttons and get what you ask for. But people aren't programmed. They're not equipped to respond as you want them to. Most of the time they don't have the answers."

"Do you think I was wrong to question people?"

"Not wrong. It was what you needed to do. But now what?"

"I don't know. I guess I'll just have to tell myself that we may never know the reason. And let it go at that."

Dad leaned back and said a little sadly, "I don't

think Diane knew, herself, why she did it. I don't think she meant to die."

"If we could only go back," Mom said, half to herself, twisting the ring on her finger.

There was silence for several seconds. Then Dr. Harris said, in a soft, gentle way, "I think you're ready to go forward, now. All of you."

During chemistry class Kevin and I spent ninety-nine percent of our time concentrating, mostly because he wanted to and I needed to. At night on the phone we talked about other things, which now meant *The Party.*

The night after our final session with the psychiatrist, I was thinking about how she'd advised me to *give it up,* only in her own words.

"Kevin," I asked, "do you think I'm compulsive?"

"Repulsive! A beautiful girl like you?"

"I said *compulsive.* What did *you* say . . . beautiful?" I laughed.

"What's so funny?"

"Kevin, come on, get real."

"Well, you *are* beautiful. Don't you ever look in a mirror?"

"Sure. When's the last time you had your eyes examined?"

"Okay, don't believe me. Listen, I've been thinking about a costume for the party, and what do you think of this idea? I could go as a garage door opener."

"A *what?*"

"I could wear a cardboard box over my head, and it

would have switches on it. When I pressed one, a flap would lift up and my face would be disguised as a car, with my glasses the headlights. What do you think of that idea?"

"Keep thinking, Kevin."

"Okay. What are you going as?"

"A cement mixer."

"Cement . . . ?"

"Kidding, just kidding. You know, the problem with getting an idea is that there're so many different routes. Like, you can be a famous person or a theme . . . you know, like an advertising slogan . . . or an inanimate object. Like a baked potato."

Kevin agreed. "I kind of like the famous person idea. Hey! I could go as Debye."

"Who?"

"You know. The guy who showed that the vibrational modes of atoms are quantized."

"Kevin?"

"Yes?"

"Keep thinking."

I was thinking, too. Thinking I might pretend I didn't know Kevin at the party.

By Wednesday he'd come up with an idea that wasn't brilliant, but not bad. He decided to go as a TV weatherman. His idea was to show all types of weather by wearing a straw hat and T-shirt for sunny and warm, a scarf, mittens, and ski boots for snow, and he'd carry an umbrella for rain, and a tiny, battery-run fan for windy weather.

"I like it," I said.

"So what have you come up with?"

"Zero."

"Oh well," Kevin said cheerfully, "no need to panic. You still have four days. No, three."

"Wonderful."

By Thursday, desperation made me decide to go as Dorothy, from *The Wizard of Oz*. Even an idea as simple as that had its drawbacks.

"Where do you suppose I could find a checked cotton dress?" I asked Mom. We were outside in the late afternoon fastening plastic covers on the deck furniture, putting flower urns away, getting ready for winter. "I know you can't make one, what with Tinker Bell's costume taking so much time."

"Well, I don't know where you'd look," Mom said. "It's a little late to find anything cotton in the stores."

"Tell me about it. They've had winter things out since July."

Suddenly, just as we were finishing, I got an idea. "Does Grandma Gwen still do volunteer work at that resale shop? For the hospital in Chicago?"

"As far as I know," Mom said, giving a final tug to the plastic cover of the outdoor grill. "Why don't you give her a call?"

"Oh, Mom, I feel a little funny about phoning for a favor. Maybe she doesn't want to stay all that close to us now."

"If that's what you think, then don't call her."

"Mo—om!" Sometimes she could be such a . . . parent!

I did call that evening, and from the way Grandma said, "Oh, Bethany, sweetheart, it's so good to hear your voice," I knew her feelings for me hadn't changed. It seemed quite natural to visit on the phone, the way we used to. Diane had once mentioned that I seemed to have more in common with Grandma than she did, the way we talked.

Tonight, after we'd caught up with one another I asked Grandma Gwen if they had anything at the resale shop that might work as a costume.

"Honey, the summer things are stored, but I could rummage around. I'm sure I can find something. I'll let you know, and perhaps you could come in Saturday to get it. When's the party?"

"Uh . . . Saturday night."

"Oh dear. Well, I'll let you know tomorrow night."

After we hung up I thought, *She won't find a cotton dress, or if she does it will be all wrong. And I won't know until Saturday which will leave me no time to find anything else, and I will therefore not go to the party.* I had to go to the party.

I could almost hear Diane saying, "Oh, don't be such a droop. It'll work out." Things usually did for her.

To my amazement, they did for me, too.

Dad drove me in to the city on Saturday morning. Grandma hugged me and murmured, "I was afraid I had lost you, too."

"Never," I said. "You can't get rid of me."

Dad asked if she saw a lot of her daughter Margo.

"Very little, in fact. She's off to Rome, Venice, who knows. She says it's on business but I have an idea it's monkey business."

Grandma showed me several cotton dresses that she

thought might work for the Dorothy costume. Then she said, "But here's something that just shouted out your name when I saw it." She opened a long, flat box and pulled out a full-length soft green dress with drapery at the top and a full skirt that also draped into folds.

"It's beautiful." I touched the filmy material. "It looks like . . . sea foam."

"Exactly." Grandma Gwen held it up to me. "It makes me think of a sea goddess, the kind that lured sailors in those Greek myths."

"The sirens," I murmured, looking down as I held the dress close. "But why did you bring it? I mean it's really lovely, but I'd have no use for it."

"I thought you might want to wear it for Halloween. You know, I don't see you as sweet, dumb Dorothy at all. This is more like something you should wear."

"I think she's right," Dad said. "Beth, you'd knock everyone's socks off if you wore this." He wanted to pay Grandma for the gown but she said, "Nonsense, it cost next to nothing."

Leaving Grandma Gwen's, I was thrilled and excited about the party for the first time. When I got home I tried on the dress. It was a little long, but Mom said she'd Scotch-tape up the hem. Since we already had cardboard and glitter for Tinker Bell's crown and wand, it took no time to cut out a small siren lyre, and cover it with sparkles.

I went over to Andrea's to get ready because her sister Elaine had all kinds of makeup and she even said she'd help us. I felt really grungy when I got there, wearing sweats and with my hair in tiny braids to make it wavy. It wouldn't have surprised me if Elaine had said, "You? A siren? Give me a break."

She didn't, though. I sat at her dressing table while she did my eyes.

"I'm not putting any blush on you, because you should look pale and alluring." She flicked a glance at Andrea. "Why are you laughing? You couldn't be pale and alluring if a million bucks was riding on it." Then to me, she said, "Okay. Don't look yet. I want to do your hair first." She undid the braids and brushed. My hair had grown; it was halfway down my back, perfect for a sea siren.

"Hey, super." Elaine studied me. "I wish, though, we had something to weave through your hair. Like tiny seashells . . . ?"

"I have some long strings of pearls in the box," I said. "Grandma loaned them to me. Actually, she said I could keep them, they're just junk."

"Super, super!" Elaine held them up, then began twining them in my hair, fastened here and there with bobby pins.

"If you're about finished," Andrea complained, "would you kindly paint the flowers on my cheeks?" She already had on her hippie outfit, complete with long straight wig and headband. "It's getting late."

Elaine sighed and turned to her sister. Over her shoulder she said to me, "Don't look yet. Put on the dress, to get the whole effect at once."

I did, and they both stared. "You look gorgeous!" Elaine said.

"Yes, you really do," Andrea agreed.

I went into the hall and looked in the full-length mirror. Was that really me? I looked so graceful in the dress. And my face, pale except for the iridescent greenish-lavender shadow on and around my eyes, and the glitter along my temples, seemed to belong to someone else. For the first time in my life I did feel beautiful.

Elaine drove us over a little early. Kevin had his own ride and Rebecca's mother would be bringing the other girls.

"I'm so nervous," Andrea said. "I hope the party's a bash, after all the work we put in today, in the barn."

"What did you do with the animals?" Elaine asked, rolling down the window and pitching out her gum. She'd given up smoking again. "Where are they supposed to stay while you guys are partying?"

"The only animals that'll be there are party animals," Andrea said. "The uncle doesn't farm. He just likes living in the country. He commutes to Chicago. He's a stockbroker."

"Oh well, another image down the tubes," Elaine said with a sigh. "Here I thought your Chris's uncle was a man of the land, out in the fields at dawn, tilling the soil. . . ."

"It's right ahead," Andrea interrupted. "See that pumpkin on the post?"

"Pumpkin? And you said he didn't farm." Elaine turned into the lane.

"He didn't grow it. Chris bought a bunch of them at the market."

Elaine pulled up into a clearing by the barn. "Looks pretty good in there," she said.

The doors had been flung open and the light coming out was a bit eerie. Andrea had said they'd strung up a lot of blue Christmas tree lights, the big kind. They'd put a few spotlights around, too, to highlight the ghosts and mummies they'd made up.

As Elaine spun the car around to leave I had an urge to run over and get back inside. I felt adrift, heading for something unknown. Instead I hurried to keep up with Andrea. "I feel a little scared," I told her.

"Oh, don't be," she said. "There'll be a lot of kids here that you know. Well, at least several. And Chris's friends are great. I told Harold about you."

I grabbed Andrea's arm to stop her. "You didn't! What did you tell him?"

"That you're a dancer, and an artist. And you're easy."

"What!"

"Kidding, just kidding. Come on."

Chris, in what I supposed was a rock musician's outfit, was still testing out the sound system. They'd rigged speakers on the beams and the music was really blasting away. At least, I thought, making conversation wouldn't be a problem. It would just be impossible.

Kids started trickling in. Most didn't wear masks, but the ones who did were so completely disguised I couldn't tell if they were people I knew or total strangers. There was a girl all in black, with a black mask. She had a patch of skin showing at her middle and there was a red hourglass painted on it, the mark of a black widow spider.

One guy was a Frankenstein monster and someone

190

else was done up as a parrot. Most of the outfits were kind of thrown together, though.

Kevin's got a lot of comment, although most kids thought he was *Sports Illustrated*.

"So? How do I look?" I finally broke down and asked him. I mean, from him I'd expected raves.

"You look beautiful," he said. "But I'm puzzled. I don't remember any part in the book where she did that."

"Which book, where who did what?"

"The Wizard of Oz. Dorothy. Did she ever play a harp?"

I stared. "Kevin. I am not Dorothy and I didn't blow in from Kansas. I am a siren, a sea goddess, an underwater sex symbol. And this is a lyre, with which I lure innocent sailors to their doom."

"Oh, then it's not a harp," Kevin said. "I really wondered about that."

"I give up," I said, and walked over and asked a gorilla to dance. Wouldn't you know, it turned out to be a girl.

After a while everyone loosened up and the party took off. Parts of costumes were taken off, too, like masks, capes, animal outfits. The kid who was a parrot ended up wearing a gym outfit with blue tights. A few feathers stuck to the back of his head but no one told him about it.

I soon tossed aside my lyre and took off the pearls that were now sagging in loops, and knotted up the sides of my skirt to make dancing easier.

I did meet Harold . . . Mac . . . and we danced a couple of times but he kept going back to some girl named Sally, and I met a Ray who was a lot of fun. And not bad looking, either.

It seemed like no time at all before cars began driving up and parents began honking for their kids. Some wandered to the door to look in, and their kids made a beeline for the cars. As the crowd thinned, the fun seemed to increase. I hoped Elaine would take her time showing up.

Ray came over just before he had to leave and asked if he could call me some time.

"Sure," I said. "Why not?" I tried to act casual, but this was the first time a guy had asked me for my phone number. They'd asked Diane all the time.

Diane. I caught my breath. *I hadn't thought about Diane once, the whole evening.*

Guilt, gray like shadows, started to creep up and take over.

No! I resisted. I didn't have to let it get hold of me. I deserved a break. I needed to start my life again. I didn't owe it to Diane to put aside all pleasure all the time.

By the time Elaine finally came and got us the party was definitely over.

"Isn't it a heartbreak," Andrea said, after she finally parted from Chris and dragged herself to the car. "To have it all end? So soon?"

"Yes, it is," I agreed. But I felt a strange lightness of spirit. It seemed to me as though my life was beginning again.

20

It's now almost a year since Diane died. That's hard to believe in some ways, but in others, it seems like more than a year. For instance, the sight of Diane lying dead on the couch downstairs is still as vivid to me as if it had happened a month ago. And yet, the feel of Diane in the house, my vision of her as a living part of the family is becoming indistinct with time. And that is so sad. I wish it were the other way around. I wish the sight of the living Diane was closer to me in memory than the other.

Our family life is basically the same and yet there's a difference of attitude. Mom still works at the hospital and Dad is still with the insurance company, but now they do other things besides work, work, work. They've taken up golf, they've joined a bowling league, and they frequently go out to dinner with friends. Sometimes we go out together, the five of us. Our family's even going to Florida for Christmas this year!

Ned has become the champion chess player of his

junior league, and Nell is taking ballet lessons. I still get annoyed sometimes at her bratty behavior, but I try to remember I wasn't perfect at her age, either. (As I am now, of course!) Ned and I have gone back to being friends. There's a quiet feeling of love between us that isn't expressed, but it's there and we both know it.

I see Steve once in a while at school. We nod to each other but never stop and talk. He split up with Heather some time ago, I hear, and is dating a freshman. Max never did come back to school. I doubt that many kids even remember him.

Andrea and Chris are definitely going together. Ray and I double with them sometimes. Ray's fun, he makes me laugh, and that's great—all I need for right now.

Kevin is still my friend, which is surprising when you consider what I put him through as a lab partner all last year.

Hope calls once in a while, even though we haven't a lot to say to each other. She sent Mom a Mother's Day card last May, just to say she was thinking of her. Mom was really touched. She's known Hope for a long time.

As for me, this past year has been strange and difficult. It's been very hard to be the only older daughter. Diane and I made up a whole. We complemented each other, we were so different. I can never fill the void she left. I don't try.

As time goes by, though, the spirit that was Diane seems to be diminishing. It's becoming harder and harder to remember how she was, especially for the little kids. They speak her name now and then but the essence of Diane seems to be fading . . . fading . . . like the memory of a dream.

I no longer even ask myself why she did it and how she could do it. She's gone. That's all. She's gone.

Tonight I'm in my room, thinking about an article I'm trying to write for the school newspaper. It's to be a feature about school spirit, a subject I admittedly know little about. I wrote a version of it, though, for an English assignment, and the teacher wants me to revise it a little for publication. I've done the first three paragraphs but at the moment I don't know how to go on.

I get up from my desk and wander about my room. It's been changed around and has new curtains and bedspreads. Andrea sleeps over every once in a while.

I stop before a framed photo of Diane. I pick it up and stare at her vivacious face. I am now the same age she was, when the picture was taken. Next year I'll be older, and I'll keep on getting older. Diane will remain the same forever, stopped in time.

Still holding the photo, I sit in the rocker she loved to sit in, and I hear myself saying, "It breaks my heart, Diane, but slowly I'm letting you go, leaving you behind. I can't take you along to wherever I'm going."

And I think of how she left this life for a reason I'll never know. She took her secret with her. Or was there one? Whatever it was, or wasn't, it was final. There was no going back, no coming back.

And now, at last, I am able to say without tears, "We miss you, Diane. We'll always miss you. You've left us with a tender ache that will never go away. But it's time to say good-bye to you and your dying. Your place is in our past. Our place is in the present."

I get up and put the photo back on the table.

Then I go to my desk, and suddenly I know what it is that I want to write. Quickly I start typing, before the thought goes away. I finish the piece, tear it out of my typewriter, and read it through. It's good! I like it!

I make a few word changes and then read it again, from beginning to end. Okay, I may never be a gee-whiz-wonderful reporter, but this isn't bad. Not bad at all. And I had fun doing it. It's something I've never done before.

Sometimes I wonder what turns my life will take, what I'll be, where I'll be. But it's enough for now to try new things while I'm young and on my way. I'm pleased. I'm forward-looking. I'm alive.

ABOUT THE AUTHOR

STELLA PEVSNER was born in Lincoln, Illinois, and attended Illinois State University and studied advertising at Northwestern. She and her husband live in a suburb of Chicago with a multitude of cats. They have four grown children, all confirmed animal lovers. Ms. Pevsner is the author of *AND YOU GIVE ME A PAIN, ELAINE, CUTE IS A FOUR-LETTER WORD, SISTER OF THE QUINTS,* and *HOW COULD YOU DO IT, DIANE?* available from Archway Paperbacks, and the Minstrel Book *ME, MY GOAT, AND MY SISTER'S WEDDING.*